The Desk

By

Jonna Turner

Cover graphic by Kevin Jones

1stBooks - rev. 04/19/02

This book is dedicated to the memory of Blanche Rathbun Munson.

Acknowledgments

Thanks to my mother, Polly Lloyd Littler, for her belief in me; to Josephine Tullos Freshour for her many years of friendship and encouragement; and to my husband, Bill, for his support and help in the plot development.

A very special thanks to my two editors: Jimmie Hylton and Sharon Frazier. I could not have done it without you.

What people are saying about *The Desk*:

In this mystery novel, events surrounding a 50-year-old murder are flashed before Jeagan Christensen's eyes when she sits at her recently acquired antique desk. Haunted by the murder scene, Jeagan travels to Memphis where her life promptly turns into a nightmare. It has to stop; and she's the only person who can make it happen.

The setting in Memphis centers on the famous Peabody Hotel. The Peabody is an old, elegant hotel in downtown Memphis and is best known for its ducks that live in the lobby fountain. The story is about two WW II lovers, one a Memphis socialite, the other a farmer's son. The scenes shift masterfully from WW II to the present. Enough to keep one guessing...This book is by local author Jonna Turner. Turner is an experienced writer in many areas. She has done technical and promotional writing and has three novels to her credit. She is currently working on a fourth.

Bill Flentje, Publisher, *Buy Colorado*, April, 2001 issue

Set in the modern day, but with haunting flashbacks to the mid-1900s, *The Desk* is a film-noir of a novel whose heroine, Jeagan Christensen, is forced by visions to become one gutsy gal in quest of answers. A piece of furniture, which comes into her possession as an antique, also brings with it the antiquity of an unrequited murder. It is the murder of an innocent, as Jeagan discovers in her quest, that was covered up to retain the honor of a class-conscious family.

Against odds, which would daunt even the seasoned professional, Jeagan rushes forth in total ignorance of her amateur stature to put meat on the bones of an old skeleton that refuses to remain in the closet. For those who like mysteries, this is one to read for sure.

Ed Beall, author of *The Skull of Bogan Rio*

Prologue

Thomas was not sure that killing the man had been the right thing to do, but the man was dead. No turning back now. Thomas scanned the area and tried not to focus on the body hidden in the shrubbery. Too well did he know what would happen if he were caught with the body of a white man. The memory of how his uncle had been lynched twelve years before still haunted his dreams.

Crack! Startled, Thomas' eyes darted to his right. For a minute he thought he saw someone watching...

"Hey, boy. Whatcha doin' out here this time of night?"

Thomas jumped. When he turned his head, he saw a uniformed policeman approaching. Sweat popped out on Thomas' face. He wiped it off with the sleeve of his black shirt.

"Uh...I's...I's awaitin' for my sistuh to get off work so's I kin walk her home, Offisuh," he said.

The policeman tapped a baton on his open palm. His eyes narrowed as he regarded the young colored man. "Where does your 'sistuh' work, boy?"

"Uh...at the hoh-tel in the kitchen," Thomas said. "She oughtta be along any minute now." Just then, he spotted two colored girls walking down Second Street toward them. *Thank you, Jesus.* "Here she come now."

The policeman turned to look at the girls. "Well, you better git on along then."

"Yessuh," Thomas said and ran toward the teenage girls.

"How y'all?" he said as he approached the girls.

Both girls grinned and stopped. "We's fine," said the taller girl.

He stood still for a moment, not sure what to do. He turned around. A block away, the policeman still watched him.

"Uh...what time is it?" Thomas asked to make conversation and keep the girls from walking away.

The taller girl—with her hair slicked back into a ponytail and wearing a red cotton dress—looked at her watch. "Near 'bout nine thirty."

"Thanks." Thomas turned around to see if the policeman was still there. He was.

"Y'all got trouble with the poh-lice?" said the shorter girl—whose curly hair stuck out from under a green-and-white bandana. "I see he's over there awatchin' you."

Thomas shrugged. "I got no trouble with the offisuh. I guess he just don't like me hangin' 'round."

"Come on and walk with us," said the shorter girl.

Thomas grinned. "Thank you kindly." He fell into step with the girls. When he looked back, he saw the policeman amble off toward Main Street twirling his baton. Relieved, Thomas slowed his pace. When the policeman was out of sight, he turned to the girls. "The poh-liceman gone now so I bes' git back."

"And, jes' what *was* you doin' over there?" said the taller girl, her hand on her hip.

"Guardin' a dead body," Thomas said straight-faced.

Both girls laughed. "Oh, you's sump'n'," the shorter girl said and slapped her knee.

Thomas said goodbye to the girls and ran back toward the body.

Chapter One

Jeagan looked up and pushed golden-brown hair away from her face.

"Good morning," said a woman—slender, blonde, and forty plus—as she settled in the aisle seat and stowed her handbag under the seat in front of her.

"Hi," Jeagan said, trying not to show her disappointment. She had hoped the seat beside her would remain empty so she could concentrate on what the next few days might bring.

"Beautiful day for a flight," the woman said.

Jeagan smiled and nodded. She looked out the window of the Boeing 727. "I hope the weather in Memphis will be this nice."

"It should be a lot warmer than Denver." The woman snapped her seatbelt into place. "Are you visiting family in Memphis?"

"No. I'm going to Memphis to do some...uh...research." Jeagan left out the part about the murder.

"How interesting," the woman said. "For a thesis or are you writing a book?"

Jeagan's midnight-blue eyes crinkled with laughter. "I graduated from the University of Colorado at Boulder several years ago, but thanks for the compliment. I'm actually doing research on...on antiques."

The woman nodded and smiled.

To make conversation, Jeagan asked, "Why are you going to Memphis?"

The woman straightened her brown tweed jacket under the seat belt. "I'm visiting my daughter and my grandson. I haven't been back to Memphis since we moved to Denver in '91." She paused. "It's nearly three years now." Tears sparkled in her eyes as she continued. "You know, it's funny how fast time goes by when you're married, but when your husband dies..." The woman laughed and pulled a tissue from her handbag to dry her eyes. "You'll have to excuse me. I go along fine for a long time and then all of a sudden, the tears start again."

"That's okay. I understand how you feel. I lost my mother two years ago, and I still miss her. And, Dad…" Jeagan frowned. "Well, that's another story."

"If your parents were as close as Jack and I were, then your dad's probably still grieving," the woman said.

Jeagan turned to look out the window as the Northwest flight pulled away from the gate. "You're probably right. Dad seems so cold and wrapped up in his own world—we can't even talk anymore." She turned to look at her seatmate again. "I don't mean to burden you with my problems."

The woman patted Jeagan's hand. "Don't apologize. I started this conversation. You know, sometimes it's easier to talk to a stranger than it is to talk to your family or friends."

Jeagan nodded. "That's true."

"Anyway, if we're going to travel eleven hundred miles together," the woman said, "we might as well know each other's name. I'm Candice Franklin."

Jeagan smiled and stuck out her hand. "Jeagan Christensen."

The women chatted while the plane taxied toward the runway and minutes later lifted off from Denver International.

*   *   *

After the flight attendants served a snack and the conversation between Jeagan and Candice lapsed, Candice pulled out a novel. She shifted into a comfortable position for the two-hour flight.

Left to her own thoughts, Jeagan relived the confrontation the night before with her dad and Brandon. After work, she had met them at Pappadeaux for dinner. She arrived after the men and found them, drinks in hand, seated on a wooden bench in the brick courtyard.

When he spotted her, Brandon Montgomery, her fiancé, pushed up the sleeve of his tailored navy suit jacket along with the cuff of his starched white shirt to check his watch. A look of disapproval wrinkled the smooth surface of his tanned face. His dark eyes cool, he leaned over and kissed Jeagan's cheek. "Late as usual," he said. "I could have played another set of doubles."

"Give her a break, Brandon," Geoff Christensen, Jeagan's father, said. He smiled and his eyes, the same color as Jeagan's, lit up when he saw his daughter. "You look wonderful, Jeag." Well over six feet, Geoff unfolded himself from the bench and stood to hug his daughter. "You look more like your mother every day."

Dressed in a short, black wool sheath with a black, lambskin coat draped around her shoulders, Jeagan smiled. "Thanks, Dad." She ignored Brandon and returned her dad's hug and nestled her face in the softness of his wool herringbone blazer. She knew her dad had lied; she did not look great. Dark circles, like smudged mascara under her eyes, gave her face a haunted look, and the loss of eight pounds, within the last two weeks, had reduced her size-six frame to near gauntness.

"Sorry I'm late," she said. "I hurried home to grab a coat. It's a lot cooler than it was this morning." A sudden gust of wind caught her shoulder-length hair, and whipped it across her face. "Let's go inside."

"Our table should be ready any minute," Geoff said. He placed his arm around his daughter's shoulder.

Brandon lagged behind. He pulled out his cell phone and dialed.

"Who are you calling?" Jeagan asked when they entered the restaurant.

"I'm checking to see if there is any word from the club. Matt and I are trying to get a court for eight in the morning."

"Do you ever play with Brandon?" Geoff asked Jeagan after the hostess showed them to a table by a window that overlooked the snow-capped Rocky Mountains in the distance—now a dusky purple outline against a tangerine winter horizon.

Jeagan looked at Brandon. "Not very often," she said. "I'm not…"

Brandon pulled out a chair for Jeagan. "I need a little more competition to keep up my game," he said.

Jeagan cut her eyes up at Brandon as he pushed in her chair.

He pulled out a chair for himself. "I mean you play a good game, but..."

"I'm not quite in your league is what you meant to say. I understand perfectly," Jeagan said icily.

"All right, kids." Geoff laughed. "Play nice."

Jeagan glared at Brandon as she accepted a menu from the waitress.

Brandon took the offered menu and opened it, unaware of Jeagan's look.

Not hungry, Jeagan quickly glanced over the menu and laid it on the table. She took a deep breath and folded her hands in her lap. "I have something to tell you both," she said.

The waitress offered Geoff a wine list.

Geoff scanned the list, ordered, and handed it back to the waitress. "What is it?" he asked, turning toward Jeagan. "A promotion?" His eyes twinkled.

"It's about time," Brandon said. "They've got her working all hours of the day and night on everything from proposals to scientific manuscripts."

Jeagan straightened in her chair and rested her forearms on the table. "No, it's not a promotion. I just wanted to tell you both that I'm going to Memphis."

"Memphis?" Brandon said.

"Whatever for?" Geoff asked. "Do you have a project to work on there?"

"No. No project. I'm going to see what I can find out about my desk and the murder I..."

"Oh, don't start that again," Brandon said. He laid his menu on the table and leaned back in his chair. "I thought you were going to take that desk back to the antique store."

The waitress returned to the table, opened a bottle of wine, and poured a sample into a wine glass.

Geoff tasted the wine. He nodded. The waitress filled each glass, then stood with her pad ready to take orders.

"Can you give us a minute?" Geoff said.

The waitress nodded. "No problem. I'll come back in a couple of minutes.

Geoff smiled. "Thanks," he said. He turned toward his daughter. "I know you've been under a lot of pressure at work and losing Mom like we did a couple of years ago..."

"It's not that, Dad." Jeagan sipped her wine and tried to stay calm. "I *have* to go to Memphis. I need to find out what's happening to me. I can't sleep. I can't work. Ever since I bought that desk..."

"Just take it back to the store and be done with it," Brandon said with exaggerated patience, as if explaining something to a child.

"I can't do that, Brandon," Jeagan said. She leaned toward him. "I need to know what's going on, and the only way I'm going to find out anything is to go to Memphis and do some research."

"But, all those things you say you saw have nothing to do with you. So why are you getting yourself all upset over something that may have happened before you were born?" Brandon asked, his voice a notch louder.

Geoff laid a hand on Brandon's arm. "Just calm down." He looked at his daughter. "Honey, I'm not trying to tell you what to do, but Brandon has a point. You don't need to get yourself all worked up about something you think you saw that you can't do anything about anyway."

"Why won't either one of you take me seriously?" Jeagan said. She hesitated for a moment and took a deep breath. "I saw a man murdered. Isn't that important?"

"You don't know what you saw," Brandon said.

"I do know what I saw, Brandon," Jeagan said. "You don't want to try to understand what I saw because it didn't happen to you. Nothing is important unless it happens directly to you."

"Oh, grow up, Jeagan," Brandon said. "You're just talking a lot of nonsense. Maybe what you saw really happened. Probably not. But, even if it did, what difference can it make to you? You don't know any of those people."

Jeagan looked to her dad for support.

Geoff took a sip of his wine. "I'm afraid he's right, honey. You need to let it go. You have your own life. You and Brandon have a wedding to plan…"

"That's it!" Jeagan pulled off her engagement ring. Tears glistened in her eyes as she laid the ring in front of her fiancé. "I'm sorry, but the engagement's off."

Brandon's eyes widened as he looked incredulously at her. "You can't mean that."

Geoff reached over and touched her shoulder. "Now, just calm down…"

Jeagan shook off her dad's hand. "I *am* calm. I'm sorry I can't be what you two want me to be." Tears slipped down her flushed cheeks. "I feel very strongly about going to Memphis. What happened *has* affected me. I may not know these people, but I *am* involved in what happened. I have to find out for myself if I actually saw that man murdered." She swiped at the tears, retrieved her handbag from the empty chair next to her, and stood. "Lorin gave me the week off to pull myself together, and I'm going to Memphis to see if I can do just that." She jerked her coat from the back of the chair and headed toward the exit.

"Jeagan!" Brandon stood and called after her.

Jeagan turned to look one last time at her dad and former fiancé. She noticed that people had turned to stare at Brandon. She saw her father place his hand on Brandon's arm and shake his head. Brandon sat down and threw his napkin on the table.

* * *

Turbulence bounced the plane and pulled Jeagan's thoughts back to the present. She took a sip from the bottle of water on her pull-down tray and wondered why the two most important men in her life could not understand and support her in her decision to go to Memphis. Instead her dad and Brandon treated her as if she were out of her mind.

Returning Brandon's ring, she told herself, was the right thing to do. He treated her like a child, continually patronizing her. She missed him, but maybe she would get over that in time. Surely. She could not and would not be treated like his incompetent kid sister. The first six months of their relationship could not have been a happier time for her. But, when Brandon's controlling, condescending nature surfaced, her stubborn and independent nature retaliated, and, she guessed, an end to the relationship was inevitable.

Her dad was another problem. She knew he loved her but since her mother's death, he had wrapped himself in a world that all but excluded Jeagan. She rarely saw him. When she did, he was warm and affectionate, but most of the time he either played golf or travelled somewhere on a business trip. Could it be that with her golden-brown hair and honey-colored skin, she reminded him too much of her mother? Surely that was not it. But, then why had he shut her out? She hurt too, but she had not excluded him from her life.

With a sigh, Jeagan realized the futility of attempting to analyze either her dad or Brandon. Besides, right now, she needed to focus on how to find evidence that would either prove or disprove that a murder took place in Memphis on July 13, 1944. And, if a murder was committed, what did her desk have to do with it?

She gazed out the window at patchy, white clouds like sheep grazing in a cobalt-blue pasture. Her thoughts drifted back to when she had found the desk three weeks earlier at Fran's Antiques on South Broadway in Denver.

*   *   *

She had searched for a writing desk for some time, but did not want a new one. An older desk with character would fit in better with the decor of her new condo in Highlands Ranch. Alone as she browsed through the shops along Broadway, she entered Fran's to the sound of a tinkling bell over the door. Immediately, she was met by the musty smell of an attic, which brought back memories of her grandmother's attic in Minneapolis.

Fran—tall, meaty, and gray-haired—greeted her with his booming voice. "Can I help you with anything, young lady?"

"Yes," Jeagan said. "I'm looking for a small writing desk." She walked across the uneven plank floor, which squeaked beneath her feet, and up to the glass counter. Inside, antique jewelry sparkled in the fluorescent display light—diamond rings in heavily filigreed silver settings that looked like something her grandmother used to wear, cameos with pink backgrounds, gold and silver broaches covered in yellowed rhinestones, and men's black onyx and sapphire rings.

Fran dropped his dust rag on the counter and wiped his hands on his apron. "Well, let's see what we have in the back that you might like." Jeagan looked around the store. Its walls, papered with honeysuckle flowers on a blue background, were dotted with gold-framed, bevelled-edged mirrors; wood-framed pictures of pastoral settings; portraits of Victorian ladies; and fruit and floral arrangements. Worn wine-colored velvet chairs, a cream-colored tapestry Victorian sofa, along with an upright piano, a cedar hope chest, and several round oak tables filled the front room of the shop.

Jeagan followed Fran through a second room filled with long oak tables of books—most with worn and tattered covers—glass goblets, gold- or floral-edged china, enamel kitchen wear, elaborate silver tea services, and kitchen odds and ends. In the back room of the shop, Jeagan noticed several oak and mahogany bookcases, some with heavy moldings and carvings, a black iron bed frame, gaily colored patchwork quilts, and an enamel-topped sideboard. Then, in a far corner, almost hidden by a large, cherry desk, she saw a small writing desk—mahogany, with a letter holder attached to the curved back.

She threaded her way through marble-topped end tables and leather-topped coffee tables. When she reached the desk, she ran her hand over the slightly scarred, dark wood and touched the curved back of the desk with the letter holder—hand-painted with blue and yellow flowers. She felt the ornate oval pulls, now dark with age, and pulled open the wide middle drawer. Again, the musty smell of an attic filled the air.

"We only got that one in yesterday," Fran said. He moved ladder-backed chairs out of his way to clear a path to the desk.

"It's perfect," Jeagan said. She smiled up at Fran.

Fran grinned. "I thought it might be," he said.

Jeagan bought the desk on the spot. Fran loaded it into her green Ford Explorer and she took it home. That was when her life had turned into a nightmare.

Chapter Two

In an effort to clear her mind of the turmoil she had left behind in Denver and the uncertainty about what lay ahead, Jeagan pulled her mind back to the present and looked out the window of the airplane. Soon, she saw the Mississippi River winding its way south toward Memphis. Green everywhere—the sunny south in March. She smiled to herself, glad to leave Denver behind, where the temperature still hovered around thirty-five. She wondered if the pants and sweaters she brought would be too heavy.

Only temporarily distracted by the scenery, questions again filled Jeagan's mind. What would she say to Isabel Lloyd if she found her? Was Isabel's fiancé really murdered on the night he proposed to her?

"Ladies and gentlemen," the Captain announced, "we're approaching Memphis International Airport. The temperature is seventy degrees."

A murmur of approval rose from the passengers. Jeagan and Candice looked at each other and smiled.

"Well, it looks like we're finally here," Candice said as she tucked her novel into her carry-on bag. "Good luck on your research."

"Thanks. I hope I can find the information I need by Saturday."

"Is that when you're returning to Denver?" Candice asked.

Jeagan nodded.

"If you get bored or lonely, call me and we'll meet for lunch. Where are you staying?"

"At the Peabody Hotel."

Candice's eyebrows arched. "Mmm. Very nice. Café Espresso there is a great place for lunch." She pulled out a business card and wrote on the back of it. "Here's my daughter's number."

Jeagan took the card. "Thanks, Candice. I'll see how my time goes."

As the plane descended, Jeagan spotted a large, silver Pyramid perched on a bluff high above the Mississippi River. The information she had found on the Internet said the architects patterned it after the pyramids near Memphis' sister city in Egypt. Seconds later, the plane passed over a bridge that formed a large, lighted M and spanned the massive River from Memphis to West Memphis, Arkansas. The plane then circled downtown where she saw the skyline with numerous glass and steel skyscrapers similar to Denver, but without the Rockies as a backdrop.

Soon Memphis International Airport, which resembled a row of tall wineglasses, came into view. When the plane landed, taxied, and parked at the gate, Jeagan retrieved her hand luggage from under the seat and stood. She smoothed the wrinkles out of her navy wool pants and cropped jacket.

"Here goes," she whispered to herself.

Outside the gate, she waved to Candice, who was greeted by her family. Jeagan then threaded her way through the crowded terminal to the baggage claim area on the ground level. The droning voice that reminded everyone not to smoke except in designated areas rang in her ears several times before she retrieved her tweed suitcase.

"Springtime," Jeagan said when a rush of warm, fragrant air enveloped her as she stepped onto the sidewalk outside the terminal. When she looked around, she spotted the shuttle from the Peabody Hotel. She had reserved a room there for two reasons—The Peabody's reputation as a grand, old southern hotel, and her investigation into the possible fifty-year-old murder would start there.

Chapter Three

The van ride revealed little of Memphis, but provided Jeagan a close-up view of the vast number of trees along the expressway.

"I wish Denver got a little more rain," she said aloud, "then we might have a few more of these beautiful trees."

"What did you say, ma'am?" the young, Asian driver said over his shoulder as he darted out of the center lane to merge the white van between two eighteen wheelers in the left lane.

Jeagan grabbed the seat in front of her. "Do you always drive like this?"

The driver grinned at her in the rearview mirror. "Sure. Haven't had wreck in ten year! I'm best and quickest driver in Memphis!"

"I'm sure you are, but would you take it easy while I'm in your van? I'd like to get to the hotel before you have accident number one. By the way, where's a good place for dinner?"

"Two, three good restaurant in hotel, but if you want true Memphis, go to Rendezvous or Pappy's on Beale Street. You get barbecue ribs at Rendezvous and red beans-n-rice at Pappy's."

"Barbecued ribs sound great. Where's the Rendezvous?"

"It downstair off alley two street from Peabody. Doorman show you. You can't miss. Smell lead you to it."

"Thanks." Her mouth began to water.

She leaned close to the window so she could see the Mississippi River from Riverside Drive after the van exited Interstate 240. The pear trees that bordered the Drive were in full pink-and-white bloom. As she watched, a massive barge churned slowly past on the River as it labored under the weight of its rusty scrap-iron cargo.

The van soon turned east off Riverside onto lower Union Avenue. Jeagan noticed the old cotton offices and warehouses along Front Street, now renovated into upscale law offices and condominiums, which still bore the cotton emblems. This area reminded her of the renovated Lower Downtown (LoDo) area in Denver. Once warehouses, the buildings had been converted into trendy restaurants and condominiums.

The van continued for a few blocks, then stopped in front of a red brick hotel that filled a city block and was shaded by green and white awnings. The uniformed doorman opened the van door for Jeagan while the driver removed her bags from the back. When she stepped out, she noticed several horse-drawn carriages parked in front of the hotel and hoped she would have time for a ride before she left Memphis. But, she immediately reminded herself that she was not here for fun.

The doorman opened the wide brass and glass doors that led into a gray marble foyer and an expansive, two-story lobby beyond. Smart shops and restaurants lined the hallway to her left and right. As Jeagan walked into the lobby area, she noticed that a grand piano stood to her right and comfortable, overstuffed chairs and sofas, along with polished tables, divided the room into scattered, softly lit conversation areas.

An ivory marble fountain, with ducks swimming around its base, dominated the center of the looby. A crowd of people surrounded the fountain, and some stood along the marble handrail on the mezzanine level above.

Jeagan walked across the plush, green oriental carpet to the front desk. "What's going on?" she asked the desk clerk.

"The Duck Master is moving the ducks back to the Skyway where they spend the night," the petite, blonde desk clerk said with a smile.

Jeagan stood on her tiptoes so she could see the Duck Master, dressed in a red military-type jacket, use a rod to gently herd the ducks. The quacking fowl climbed out of the fountain, waddled slowly along a red carpet that had been rolled out across the lobby, and entered an elevator. Laughter and a round of applause filled the air as the brass doors closed on the famous ducks.

Jeagan, smiling, turned toward the desk clerk.

"The ducks will come down again in the morning at eleven to spend the day in the fountain," the clerk said. "It's a tradition that's been going on for years. In fact, it's the hotel's trademark."

"I read about that on your web site," Jeagan said and gazed around the gracious lobby while the clerk finished the paperwork. Jeagan admired the scrollwork on the two-story marble columns, the pastoral paintings that decorated the cherry-paneled walls, the grandfather clock that ticked quietly nearby, and the massive chandeliers that hung from the carved ceiling above the mezzanine level.

"Miss Christensen, you're in room 1004. I'll have a bellman take your bags up for you." The desk clerk tapped a bell nearby on the counter. Presently, a slightly stooped, gray-haired bellman appeared from nowhere. "Enjoy your stay," the desk clerk said. She handed Jeagan's room key to the bellman.

"Thank you." Jeagan followed the gray-haired man, dressed in a black-and-red uniform, to the elevators across the lobby. The crowd, she noticed, had meandered off in various directions now that the ducks were out of sight.

One young couple stood out from the rest—hand in hand and obviously very much in love. A dull ache shot through Jeagan's heart as she entered the elevator. She missed Brandon. No, maybe not Brandon, but what she wished they could have together.

Jeagan and the bellman rode the elevator to the tenth floor in silence. She entered her room after he unlocked it, handed her the key, and set her two bags on the floor. How inviting and restful, she thought as she looked around the room. She thanked the bellman and handed him a tip.

When she had the room to herself, she admired the subdued blue-floral bedspread with matching, floor-length drapes drawn back now to expose ivory sheers and large windows that overlooked the River.

What a lovely room to share with someone you loved, she thought, and then stopped herself. She would not let herself think

14

about Brandon now. After all, they had spent the last two months in one argument after another, which showed her that they were probably incompatible anyway.

Enough of that, there was work to do. But, first she would change into something cooler, her lightweight black slacks, a white cotton shirt, and lemon-colored blazer, and then try out the ribs at the Rendezvous.

After she changed, she checked her slim, five-foot-eight reflection in the mirror and pinched her cheeks to give her face some color. She studied her normally tanned face, now pale and drawn, while doubts about herself and her mission resurfaced. A detective she was not—only a technical writer at Caldwell & Ottonello Engineers in the Denver Tech Center. Her job as an environmental proposal writer certainly provided her no experience in how to be a private detective. She felt much more comfortable describing hazardous and radiological waste sites than she did nosing into something that was really none of her business.

As she left her room, Jeagan wondered where the next few days would take her and if she would be able to find out if her desk had come from this hotel and if Isabel Lloyd and her family had stayed in the Peabody on July 13, 1944. If these things were true, then she was one step closer to finding out if Alan McCarter was killed that night.

Chapter Four

With the help of the doorman, Jeagan soon found the Rendezvous restaurant tucked into a nearby alley. She descended the steep stairs and inhaled the aroma of freshly cooked pork.

"I'll have a half order of the dry ribs," Jeagan told the black waiter after she was seated and had looked over the menu. He scrawled her order on his pad and left her to observe her surroundings. The place definitely had atmosphere.

The cellar restaurant was decorated with memorabilia from years long past—old Coke trays and magazine ads were displayed on the brick walls alongside autographed pictures of movie stars—Elvis, Marilyn Monroe, Frank Sinatra—politicians, and musicians. Street signs from a younger Memphis also dotted the walls. Photos of Riverside Drive, apparently taken around the time when cotton was big business, showed men loading bales of cotton onto paddle wheel riverboats. There were also photos of horse-drawn carriages that rolled down what used to be cobblestoned Main Street but was now Mid-America Mall.

Jeagan sipped white wine while she waited for her dinner. The other diners, she noticed, were mostly men. Probably in town on business, she thought, since it was a Monday night.

After she ate half of her dinner and cleaned the barbecue sauce from her hands and face, she climbed the steps to the alley and, nervous about what she had to do, decided to take the long way back to the hotel. She circled the block, which took her along Madison Avenue to Monroe where she noticed old brick and stone buildings, newly renovated, which still bore the dates of their original construction— 1906, 1895, 1901. These, mixed with the newer, more modern glass-and-steel architecture gave the area an eclectic feel similar to Denver's downtown business district.

Jeagan arrived back at the hotel as the rays of the pink and purple sunset blanketed Union Avenue and the River beyond.

Years fell away from the faces of the old buildings now bathed in the evening light.

Minutes later, back in the hotel lobby, she took a deep breath, squared her shoulders, and approached the front desk. It was time to begin her search for a possible killer. She asked to speak to the manager.

"Is something wrong, ma'am?" the desk clerk asked, a worried expression on her face.

"No," Jeagan said. "I'm doing research and I'd like to ask the manager a couple of questions."

"Oh." The petite, blonde clerk smiled and leaned on the counter. "Are you writing a book? You know John Grisham wrote a book set in Memphis, and they filmed part of it here. I got to meet Tom Cruise when they filmed a few of the scenes at the hotel. Boy, is he a hunk."

"No, sorry," Jeagan said. "I'm only doing research on...uh...antiques."

"Oh, okay." The clerk seemed to lose interest in Jeagan's mission and excused herself to look for the manager.

Soon, a middle-aged, partially bald man appeared from a doorway behind the front desk. He seemed preoccupied but greeted Jeagan courteously. "I'm Bryan Yust. How can I help you?"

"I'd like to find out about a desk that I bought at an antique store in Denver," Jeagan said. "The dealer gave me the name of the owner who said she bought the desk here in the late seventies when the hotel was renovated. Would you have any records that date back that far?"

"I'm not sure, Miss...?"

"Excuse me." She extended her hand. "I'm Jeagan Christensen." She paused. "Look, I know this sounds crazy, but I need to find out if the desk I bought was in this hotel in 1944 and if it was in room 807."

"Well...Miss Christensen, I doubt if our archived records will show where your desk was located even if we could find out if it actually came from this hotel."

17

Not about to give up that easily, Jeagan continued. "I know it's a lot to ask and it was a long time ago, but don't you have some records somewhere of the items sold at the auction during the renovation? Maybe the records are stored somewhere on microfiche. If you could point me in the general direction, I'll do all the research myself."

"I don't know." Bryan Yust scratched his head and removed his glasses, as if to stall for time to think. After a few moments, he returned his glasses to their place on his nose. "Let me check with our accountant. I won't be able to reach him this evening, but I'll see what I can do in the morning. Will that help?"

"Yes. Thanks," Jeagan said. "I appreciate anything you can do to get me permission to look at the records."

"Excuse me for asking, but why do you want to find out about your particular desk?"

"I'm…uh…interested in antiques and their history," Jeagan said. "You might call it a new hobby."

"Well, I'll let you know what I find out in the morning. Good night." Yust walked behind the counter and into his office.

With nothing in particular to do, Jeagan roamed the lobby and looked in the windows of the smart gallery shops. Peabody designer items were displayed with the famous duck emblem: brightly colored golf shirts, sweaters, ladies' sportswear, jewelry, books, and stationery.

She looked up and noticed a few people on the mezzanine and climbed the curved, white marble staircase on the right side of the lobby to have a look around. Tucked into a quiet nook, set back from the elevator, she found a dark, paneled history room. Glass cases displayed old photos and memorabilia from days gone by, which included tableware and pictures of couples as they danced in the Skyway Ballroom in the forties.

After a few minutes, she decided to go back to her room to try to get some sleep. The search had begun. Now, all she could do was wait until she heard from the hotel manager. Hopefully, he could obtain permission for her to search through the old records. If not, she would have to go to Plan B, if she could come up with a Plan B.

Chapter Five

Jeagan slept fitfully. When she awoke and got out of bed the next morning, she stretched and walked over to the window. It was a bright, sunny morning with a light mist still hugging the mighty River. A few early risers, she noted guiltily, were out for a run.

In the morning light, doubts again crept into Jeagan's mind. Maybe she had wasted time and money traveling here to look into a possible murder that may or may not have happened in 1944 and had nothing to do with her.

*   *   *

Her life had been so predictable, what an awful word, before she had brought the desk home from Fran's Antiques. She had found the perfect spot for the desk in her bedroom, placed it there, and cleaned and polished it until it gleamed softly in the reflection from her double windows. After she had placed some of her favorite books and a silver-framed picture of her parents on top, the desk blended in well with the antique armoire and the white, iron-framed bed. Everything was perfect until the next day when she sat down at her new desk to put stationery and a few letters into the single drawer.

As soon as she sat down, her head started to spin. She folded her arms on the desk, lowered her head, and closed her eyes, in hopes that the dizzy spell would pass. While her eyes were closed, she heard voices. Jeagan gasped as a sunny room came into view. The room was papered with yellow floral wallpaper and furnished with twin beds covered in soft, yellow-and-white chenille spreads. White, filmy drapes were drawn back from a double window. In the room, she saw a young woman—her long, glossy dark hair pulled away from her face with tortoise-shell combs. The young woman—slim and lightly tanned—was dressed in a pale blue voile dress with a scooped neck and short, puffy sleeves. She sat at a writing desk identical to Jeagan's and appeared to be writing a letter.

Jeagan heard a stern, matronly voice call out from an open doorway beyond the desk. "Isabel, hurry or we'll be late for dinner...Isabel, did you hear what I said? You can finish your letter later. Who are you writing to anyway?"

"Oh, just Virginia White, mother. I...I wanted to say hello and see if she's enjoying her summer vacation in Alabama," the clear voice of the young woman responded. "I'll be right there."

Jeagan lifted her head as the images faded. Her heart thudded inside her chest. Confused and somewhat disoriented, she had no idea what she had seen. Whatever it was, it looked like footage from an old movie.

*   *   *

The sound of the telephone brought Jeagan back to the present. She walked over to the nightstand to pick it up. "Hello?" she answered expectantly. "Oh, good morning, Mr. Yust."

"Good morning, Miss Christensen," Bryan Yust said. "I hope I didn't wake you."

"No. I was already awake," Jeagan said. "Have you been able to talk to the accountant?"

"Not exactly. I found out that he's out of town and won't be back until the end of the week." Yust hesitated. "But, I left word for him at his hotel to call me."

Disappointment edged Jeagan's voice. "Do you think he might return your call today?"

"I can't say, but I'll let you know as soon as I hear from him."

"Well, thank you for your help." Jeagan had to find out something before the end of the week. She did not want to wait that long, but what could she do? There was nowhere else to begin her search. This was the only logical place to start. She already knew that an Isabel Lloyd lived in Memphis, according to directory assistance. Whether or not it was the right one was something else. But, there was no record of the death of an Alan McCarter on July 13, 1944. Her cousin in Denver, who was a detective with the Denver Police Department, had confirmed this for her through Shelby County Vital Statistics in Memphis.

Breakfast. That's what she needed, especially hot coffee. Hot coffee would help her wake up and sort out what to do until the end of the week, if the accountant did not return Mr. Yust's call.

Jeagan showered, dressed, and rode the elevator to the lobby. To her left and around the corner among the upscale shops, she found the hotel's art-deco Café Espresso. She waited only a few minutes and then was seated at a black table-for-two. A waitress brought hot coffee while Jeagan glanced over the menu. After she placed her order, she looked through the local morning newspaper. Isn't there ever any good news to print, she wondered idly? Deficit, taxes, inflation, old wars still raging, drive-by shootings…The problems never seemed to change, only the locations.

She sipped the strong, hot coffee, ate a croissant with raspberry preserves, and considered her situation. The key was to find out if her desk was in this hotel in July 1944 and if it was in room 807. If this were true, then she would try to find out if Isabel Lloyd was in that room that summer. Jeagan was almost afraid to learn the answers to these questions. If the answers were all affirmative, she had a grave responsibility ahead of her.

Thirty minutes later, she folded her newspaper and stood to leave the restaurant. A sudden chill crept up her spine; she felt uneasy, as if someone were watching her. She turned around and noticed that most of the couples in the restaurant talked quietly. The people who sat alone were either busy eating or reading the newspaper. No one is watching me, she thought. I'm jumpy and anxious to get this done and go home.

Jeagan left the restaurant through the door that opened onto Second Street. She strolled along the sidewalk and idly picked a white pear blossom from one of the trees that lined the street. The petals felt like silk against her skin. When she reached the end of the block, she turned and continued her walk toward Beale Street—similar to Bourbon Street in New Orleans.

Beale Street—with its old dry goods stores, shoe stores, clothiers, and tailor shops now converted to restaurants, antique shops, retailers, and nightclubs—was quiet at this time of morning. But, according to the doorman, it was a lively nightspot with good food and great blues bands.

When she reached W.C. Handy Park, she sat on a green, wooden bench.

"What should I do?" she asked a pigeon that waddled toward her on the concrete sidewalk, obviously in search of a hand out. The pigeon cooed and bobbed its head.

"You're no help," Jeagan said. She leaned back and settled herself on the bench. Her first instinct was to try to contact Isabel Lloyd, but first she had to confirm that Isabel and her family were actually in the hotel in July of 1944. If Jeagan could only verify that they were there and that her desk had been in their room…

"I wonder," Jeagan said aloud, as an idea formed in her mind. The gray-haired bellman. How long had he been at the Peabody, she wondered. If she could talk with him for a few minutes, he might know something that could help her, or he might be able to tell her where she could find some old hotel records. With a plan in mind, she rose from the bench and headed back to the hotel.

Chapter Six

Jeagan approached the front desk. "Excuse me," she said.

The thirtyish, black desk clerk looked up. "May I help you?"

"Yes…I…Do you know if the bellman who was on duty yesterday around four is here today? He was an older man with silver hair."

"Oh, you mean Mr. Hobbs. Yes, he's here. In fact, he just took someone's bags out to a taxi. He'll be back in a minute. Is there something you needed?"

"No…I…Thank you."

Jeagan turned and walked toward the doors that led to Union Avenue. She watched Mr. Hobbs load bags into a taxi. When he finished, she opened the door and walked toward him.

"Mr. Hobbs?" She stepped into his path. "Uh…I'm Jeagan Christensen, a guest here." She shaded her eyes from the morning sun. "You might remember me. You carried my bags to my room yesterday afternoon."

"Oh, yes, Miss Christensen, I remember. How are you this morning?" He tipped his hat and his lined face lit in a smile.

"I'm fine, thank you. Uh…could I ask you a question?" Jeagan said. She stuffed her hands into the pockets of her olive wool slacks to keep them from shaking.

"Why, sure you can. What can I do for you?" he asked.

"How long have you worked at this hotel?" she asked.

"Oh, now let me see." His age-spotted brow wrinkled in concentration. "Since 1940. Yes, that's it, 1940."

"Great! Then maybe you can help me." She backed toward the building and out of the line of sidewalk traffic. Mr. Hobbs followed her, a puzzled look on his face.

"Do you think you can remember back to 1944?" Jeagan said.

"I'm sure I can, but that was long before you were born. What is it you want to know?" he said.

"Well, I recently bought an antique desk, and I was told it originally came from this hotel. I'd like to verify that."

Mr. Hobbs rubbed his chin. "Well, I know there were desks in all of the rooms back then, but whether or not your desk came from here...Have you talked to the hotel manager?"

"Yes. I talked with Mr. Yust earlier. He said he would get in touch with the hotel accountant to see if he could help me, but the accountant is out of town. I hoped he might have some old records on microfiche or something that I could look at."

"I don't know about any microfiche, but I do know there are some old records stored in the basement, but you'd have to get a key from Mr. Yust to get in there."

"Thank you, Mr. Hobbs." Jeagan smiled and patted his arm. "You've been a big help."

"Well, anytime, ma'am." Mr. Hobbs nodded and entered the hotel.

Jeagan remained on the sidewalk. She knew what she had to do—go to the basement unobserved and find the storage room. But, first she had to find something cooler to wear. The wool sweater and pants she wore were too hot. She decided to try the shops inside the hotel.

An hour later, Jeagan returned to her room with new lightweight outfits—a two-piece jungle print dress, khaki slacks with a striped orange-and-khaki shirt, and jeans and a Peabody tee shirt with ducks marching across the front. She changed into the khaki pants and striped shirt. Cooler, she was now ready to explore the basement.

As Jeagan picked up her room key to leave the room, the phone rang. She answered it, annoyed at the delay. "Hello?"

"Jeagan?" It was Brandon.

Her face lit in a smile. "Brandon! I've missed—"

He cut her short. "When are you coming home?"

Her smile quickly faded. "Not until I find out about my desk," she said, irritated at his harshness. "Anyway, how did you know where to find me?"

"The receptionist at your office told me," he said. "Jeagan, don't you think you've carried this business too far? Why don't you come home and sell that desk so our lives can get back to normal?"

"No, I'm not coming home. Brandon, we had this argument two days ago. I know what I'm doing. I know you don't believe what I told you about the experiences I've had since I bought the desk, but they did happen and I have to find out why."

"Jeagan, stop being ridiculous." Exasperation tinged his voice. Brandon continued. "You've really let your imagination run away with you, you know that?"

"I'm not letting my imagination run away with me, Brandon. The daydreams, or flashes from the past, or whatever I had happened for a reason, and I want to know what it is."

"You're acting like an irrational child."

"I'm very rational, Brandon," Jeagan said calmly, trying not to lose her temper. "I'm not a child, and I'd appreciate it if you'd stop treating me like one."

"Jeagan, listen to me…"

Jeagan sighed, then laughed dryly. "No, Brandon. My listening to you days are over."

"You don't really mean that. You're just upset."

"Oh, but I do mean that. Bye, Brandon." Jeagan dropped the phone into the cradle. Tears stung her eyes as she sat on the bed, feeling empty and alone. Maybe it was hard for Brandon and her dad to believe what had happened to her since she bought the desk, but if they loved her as they claimed, then they should try to help her, not treat her as if she were out of her mind.

"Maybe I am out of my mind," Jeagan said as she recalled the second incident that occurred after she brought the desk home. The second was more frightening than the first.

*   *   *

Two days after the first incident, she had sat at the desk to write a check when she had once again become dizzy and had

26

put her head down for a moment, in hopes the dizziness would pass. This time, she saw a dark door with the number 807 on it. It silently opened and she saw two people inside, in what appeared to be a sitting room. The furniture, upholstered in wine-colored velvet and creamy tapestry, appeared to be Victorian. Crystal table lamps cast a soft glow on the wallpaper with wine-colored flowers sprinkled across it and a cream-colored floral carpet. A man and a young woman were alone in the room.

"Isabel, I forbid you to see that boy again!" the man said. He stood facing a heavily draped window with his hands clasped behind his back. Of average build and height, he wore a dark suit with a faint white stripe and his hair was slicked back from his face.

The young woman appeared to be the same as before—Isabel. She sat in a tapestry Queen Anne chair. Her dark hair was pulled back with a dove-gray ribbon that matched her short-sleeved, polished cotton dress and gentle eyes. The dress, with padded shoulders and wide lapels, resembled the style of clothes Jeagan's grandmother had worn at about the same age. Jeagan noticed the delicate beauty of the woman's face.

Isabel looked up at the man. Tears sparkled in her dark eyes. "But, he loves me, Father, and I love him. He's a kind, gentle, intelligent person. There's no reason for us not to be together."

"You're too young for a relationship with any young man, Isabel. And, when the time comes for you to marry, you'll choose someone from our social circle, not someone like Alan McCarter. He can offer you nothing but poverty."

"Alan can offer me plenty!" Isabel said, her cheeks flushed in anger. "He'll finish law school after the war's over and then practice here in Memphis. I'm very proud of him, and you could be too if you'd give him half a chance."

The man turned slowly to face Isabel. "No daughter of mine is going to marry some backwoods white trash. I don't care what he studies at the university. The matter is closed, Isabel," he said with finality.

"No. It isn't!" Isabel screamed and ran from the room. The door slammed behind her.

Jeagan remembered how upset she had been after the images had faded. Again, she had wondered what was happening to her. Her daydream or whatever it was, made her feel she had witnessed events that happened many years earlier. She clearly saw the navy suit that Isabel's father wore, the deep wine color of the sofa, and Isabel's gray cotton dress, all out of another era—another place in time.

Two days later, Jeagan invited her dad and Brandon over for Sunday brunch and showed them her new desk. Geoff sat at the desk and ran his hand over the top and legs. "Nice desk. Seems to be in pretty good shape," he had said.

Jeagan watched him closely to see if anything happened to him. He stood up from the desk with no apparent dizziness. Next, she asked Brandon to sit at the desk. He did but nothing happened. His only comment was to ask Jeagan how much she had paid for the desk.

Over lunch of an omelette, hashbrowns, and a green salad, Jeagan related her first two experiences to Brandon and her dad. Her dad patted her on the head and told her that she was working too hard and reading too much science fiction. Brandon abruptly insisted she return the desk to the antique shop without delay and stop her silly nonsense.

*   *   *

"Well," Jeagan said aloud, as she stood and brought her thoughts back to the present, "Brandon has made it perfectly clear how he feels." With that, she left her room and let the door slam behind her. There was work to do in the basement.

Chapter Seven

Jeagan entered an empty elevator and hoped it would stay that way until she reached the basement. But, on the eighth floor, the elevator stopped and a middle-aged couple got on. The pair greeted Jeagan politely and then entered into a conversation about where to have dinner that night.

"Let's go out to Corky's. I hear their barbeque is as good as…" Moments later, the elevator door opened on the first floor and the couple got out. Jeagan held her breath as two men crossed the lobby toward the elevator, but the doors closed before they reached it.

When the elevator stopped on the basement level, Jeagan stepped off and walked down the hallway. The basement contained a workout center, a massage room, and several offices, but no storage area. She watched through a glass wall as men and a few women—dressed in shorts and tee shirts—lifted weights and walked on treadmills. Disappointed, Jeagan realized that if archived files were kept in any of the offices on this floor, she would never be able to get to them with so many people around. It appeared she would have to wait until the accountant returned Mr. Yust's call.

Jeagan headed toward the elevator feeling defeated. As she lifted her hand to press the up button, she noticed a door to her left marked Stairs. She looked through the glass window and saw a stairway that went down as well as up— a sub-basement. Jeagan glanced down the hallway. A man walked toward her but then turned and entered the workout room. After the door closed behind him, she quietly opened the door to the stairwell and slipped inside.

When she reached the lower basement, she looked up and down the hall, at a loss where to start her search, especially in the dim light from low-wattage bulbs that hung at wide intervals along the low ceiling. Unmarked white doors, all closed, lined both sides of the concrete hallway. With no identifying signs on the doors, there was no other choice but to check each room until she—hopefully—found the records storage area. If anyone comes along, I'll say…What will I say, she wondered? She would have to cross that bridge when she came to it.

Jeagan tried the first two doors with no luck. They were locked tight. The third door opened onto a storage room with mops, brooms, cleaning supplies, and cans of air freshener that lined the metal shelves. The next door opened onto what appeared to be the hotel telephone system with thin, plastic-coated wires and circuits that covered a gray wall panel. After that, all the doors on that end of the hall were locked. Jeagan retraced her steps and passed the stairs where she tried doors on the other end of the hall. The first three doors were securely locked; the next was unlocked and only revealed shelves half-filled with folded bedspreads, sheets, pillowcases, towels, wash cloths, and bath mats. Farther back in the room sat a row of washers and dryers. She closed the door and tried the handle on the next door. It would not turn, but the whole lock mechanism jiggled as if loose. Maybe a good push would loosen it further. Jeagan gave the door her best hip action but it still held.

She must have been dreaming to think she could find or get into the hotel records down here. Management would never leave their records in an unlocked area. Half-heartedly, she tried the rest of the doors until she reached the end of the corridor. All were secure.

"Rats!" As she headed back to the elevators, Jeagan gave the door with the loose lock a kick to relieve her aggravation. The door shot open and banged against the wall. She gasped in surprise and looked around to make sure no one had seen her kick the door. The hallway was empty. When she grabbed the door handle, she noticed that it now turned in her hand. The door had been locked when she tried it minutes earlier, she was sure of that.

Jeagan entered the room. In the dim light from the hallway, she saw gray metal file cabinets that stood in neat rows down the length of the room. Quietly, she closed the door and turned on the light in the windowless room. Her heart pounded in her ears; her hands shook. She checked the label on the first cabinet. The neatly typed white card on the top drawer read: Purchase Orders, 1990, 500000-500600. Bingo! This might be the place to find the information she needed. Jeagan walked down the rows of cabinets and read the date on the first cabinet in each row: 1980, 1970, 1960, 1950, and finally a yellowed card on the next row read 1940.

Jeagan held her breath and pulled on the top drawer. It wouldn't budge. "Locked!" she spat out and banged her hand on the top of the cabinet. The sound echoed eerily in the long, cement-block room. Jeagan shivered. The room was damp and musty and she was getting nowhere fast.

"Hey, Harold!"

Jeagan jumped as she heard a man's voice in the hall. She would be caught any minute.

"What did you do with the new bedspreads for the third floor?" the man said. "Mr. Yust said you signed for them this morning, and he wants them put out before the convention crowd gets here this afternoon."

The owner of the voice stood directly in front of the door. Jeagan held her breath and expected the door to open any minute. Soon, she heard another voice that sounded as if it came from farther down the hall. The fading sound of footsteps told her that the man talking to Harold was moving away from her.

Jeagan took a deep breath and decided it was a good time to get out of the basement— before she was caught. She turned to leave. "Ouch!" she cried, as her elbow scraped across a round knob on the file cabinet. She twisted her arm to inspect the scratch. No blood. She rubbed the spot vigorously and then looked closely at the grooved knob. When she pushed on it, a sharp *click* sounded from inside the cabinet. Jeagan pulled the handle. The drawer slid out, grinding slightly.

"Yes!" Jeagan whispered. She flipped through the folders and read the labels. Carpets...Rugs... Housekeeping... Maintenance... Light Fixtures... Plants. There seemed to be no particular order to the folder titles. She pulled out the next drawer. Kitchen... Dining Rooms... Skyway... Furniture!

Jeagan jerked the folder out of the drawer. "All right!"

Screech! She jumped.

The spine-chilling sound of metal scraping on concrete came from the other end of the room. For a moment, she was too scared to move. Her heart pounded in her ears. She inhaled deeply and gathered her courage. Quietly, she closed the drawer, stuffed the folder inside her shirt, stood on her tiptoes, and looked over the cabinets to the other end of the room. No one appeared to be there. She bolted. When she reached the door, she grabbed the handle, jerked it open, and slammed it behind her. She ran down the hall toward the stairwell. She encountered no one before she reached the stairs where she threw open the door and raced up to the basement level. When she reached the basement, she quietly opened the door and looked down the hall. A man dressed in gray shorts and a white tee shirt entered the hall from the workout room. He turned in the opposite direction.

Jeagan stepped into the hall and pushed the up button on the elevator. Moments later, she jumped as the door to the workout room opened and two women walked out. The women—one dressed in black spandex shorts and top and the other in red spandex—blotted their faces and chests with towels draped around their necks. They spoke quietly as they approached the elevator.

"How about tennis at the Racquet Club after our meeting this afternoon?" the thirty-ish blonde with a short, tight body said to her friend. The woman smiled at Jeagan as they joined her in front of the elevator.

Jeagan returned the smile and managed a forced, "Hello."

The second woman, brunette and slightly older, her body tanned and toned, nodded to Jeagan. "Don't you have to have a membership before you can play there?" she said to her friend.

Calm down, Jeagan told herself as the three women waited for the elevator. Beads of perspiration trickled down Jeagan's neck. A towel to blot her neck would be welcome about now.

She kept her eyes on the door to the sub-basement, afraid that at any minute someone would come through the door and accuse her of breaking and entering—and theft.

"Yes, you do have to have a membership," the blonde said. The elevator arrived noiselessly and the three women stepped inside. "Nicki Speck in Lefler's office said we could be her guests at the club."

Do these women have any idea that they are on the elevator with a thief, Jeagan wondered?

The women got off on the sixth floor. Jeagan pressed the close button and leaned back against the wall of the elevator.

Chapter Eight

Minutes later, when Jeagan was back in her room with the door securely fastened and the chain lock in place, she opened the miniature refrigerator. Glass bottles clinked together as she searched for something to calm her nerves. A bottle of white wine would do. After she poured half a glass, she dropped into a chair and took a long drink. She held the glass in both hands, closed her eyes, and laid her head against the back of the chair.

When her heart slowed somewhat, she opened her eyes, stood, and walked over to the windows. People on the street hurried here and there, oblivious to the fact that she could quite possibly have been caught in the act of breaking and entering, or she could have been mugged or raped, if the sound she heard in the basement was not made by a hotel employee. If it had been one of the hotel staff she heard in the room with her, they would have confronted her most likely and had her arrested on the spot.

Cold fear crept up her back. Scared and unsure of what to do next, Jeagan paced the room, drink in hand. She wondered whether she should call her dad or call the airline and book the next flight back to Denver. The folder. That, she reasoned, could be disposed of quite easily somewhere away from the hotel.

"Calm down," she told herself. "No one is following you." That sound, she rationalized, could have been made by a rat or something falling. The building is old and must creak and groan a lot, she thought. She set the glass on the nightstand. Somewhat calmer now, she would make no plans for retreat yet. After all, she had travelled eleven hundred miles, done considerable damage to her savings account, and needed to find answers to the questions that filled her mind, such as: why me? She wondered why all these incredible glimpses into what she believed was someone else's past had been given to her and why she felt compelled to do something about them.

* * *

Jeagan vividly recalled the third incident that occurred after she had bought the desk. She had avoided sitting at the desk after the first two incidents, and because neither her dad nor Brandon had experienced anything unusual when they sat at the desk and did not believe what had happened to her, she had begun to doubt it herself.

A week after the second incident, Jeagan gathered her courage and sat at the desk again. She needed to find out if what had happened to her previously was real or only in her imagination. As soon as she was seated, her head began to spin. Again, she lowered her head. In a few moments, her eyes closed, she saw a city park—Court Square according to a bronze plaque at the entrance. A tiered, bronze water fountain with a round, brick base stood in the center of the park, surrounded by a brick terrace. Several gravel paths lead away from the round fountain through oak trees; one path led toward a large, white gazebo set among giant, dark green azalea shrubs. In the gazebo, she saw a young man and a young woman—again, it was Isabel—who sat on the gray bench that ran around the interior of the gazebo. The couple held hands and faced each other.

"Isabel," Jeagan heard the young man say tenderly, "Will you wait for me and marry me when the war's over?" Jeagan noticed the formal white uniform the young man wore. He must be a naval officer, she thought.

"Of course, Alan," Isabel said, her face aglow. "You know I'll wait for you. I'm not going anywhere."

Jeagan watched the dark-haired young man reach over and touch Isabel's cheek and cup her face in his hand.

"I'm so lucky to have someone as beautiful as you," Alan said. "I'll do everything I can to make you happy."

Isabel reached up and held Alan's hand. "I'm already happy. I just wish the war was over now so we could get married." Isabel snuggled against Alan's chest and then glanced at her watch. "Alan, I have to get back to the Peabody. It's nearly nine. My father doesn't know where I am and if he finds out…"

"Can't you stay a little longer?" Alan pleaded his case. "I may not see you again for a long time."

"No. I'm sorry, Alan. Father's business meeting will be over soon, and he'll wonder where I am. I promise I'll write to you everyday and pray for you...and wait for you to come back." Tears streaked Isabel's cheeks as she stood to leave.

"I'll write you as often as I can, sweetheart." Alan looked up at Isabel as if his heart were about to break. "Please don't forget me and don't stop loving me."

"I won't."

"The war should be over soon," Alan said, as if to convince himself. "Hitler's own men have turned against him, so it can't last much longer. I know I'll be back soon."

Alan stood and took Isabel into his arms and kissed her passionately. He then held her for a long moment until she broke away and ran toward the hotel. Alan slumped back onto the bench.

Jeagan watched the scene unfold. Her heart ached for the young couple. Beside Alan, she noticed a newspaper. The city and date on it were clearly visible— Memphis, Tennessee; July 13, 1944!

Suddenly Alan jumped to his feet, as an older man approached. "Good evening, Mr. Lloyd," Alan said to Isabel's father.

"Let's get one thing straight, McCarter, and then I don't ever want to see you again." Lloyd's voice shook with fury. "Stay away from my daughter or I'll kill you."

Alan stood his ground. "I don't care what you say, I will marry Isabel when I get back."

"That's not likely," Lloyd said. Hate burned in his eyes.

"If you'd only listen to reason, Mr. Lloyd," Alan raised his hands for emphasis. "When I finish law school, I'll be able to give Isabel a nice home and..."

"I warned you, McCarter, but you won't listen." With that, Lloyd pulled a black pistol from inside his coat. He fired twice.

A look of disbelief on his face, Alan stumbled backward onto the railing and collapsed on the gray, wooden floor. He gasped for air as blood trickled from his mouth. Jeagan watched in horror as Alan's life ebbed away.

When Alan choked his last bloody breath moments later, Lloyd looked around. The park was empty; he whistled. Soon a tall, gangly, black teenager appeared at his side and helped him drag Alan's body down the stairs of the gazebo into the nearby shrubbery.

"I'll get the car, Thomas," Lloyd said. "You stay here and make sure no one sees the body. I won't be long. We'll load him in the trunk and take him down to the River."

Thomas nodded and sat on the gray gazebo steps. He trembled slightly; his large, dark eyes scanned the park. He jumped as a couple, hand in hand, strolled by on the street toward the park, but took a path away from the gazebo. The couple had obviously not heard the shots.

Jeagan moved slightly and heard a scraping sound behind her. Thomas turned and looked in her direction, his eyes—cold and piercing—seemed to look right through her.

The next thing Jeagan knew, she found herself on the floor of her bedroom. The chair was overturned and lay beside her. She pulled herself up, still somewhat dizzy and disoriented. Then, when she realized what she had seen, she fell across her bed and sobbed uncontrollably.

"Dear God in Heaven, what's happening to me? And, that poor man...I saw him killed! Cold-blooded murder! How could Isabel's father do that?"

Exhausted, Jeagan soon cried herself into a fitful sleep. When she awoke several hours later, she sat up and called her dad. His voice mail answered after several rings. "He must be on the golf course," she said, as she looked at her watch and replaced the receiver. If only Mom were still alive, she thought. I could talk to her and she would believe me and try to help. Tears formed in Jeagan's eyes again, but she wiped them away. She knew that talking to her dad or Brandon would do her no good. They hadn't believed her before and would never believe this.

"No," she had told herself. "I'll have to work this out for myself. I could take the desk back to the antique store and, hopefully, be rid of—whatever it is— that's happening to me." But, she knew she would not return the desk.

The next day, she went to work as usual. Two hours after she sat at her desk, she had not written the first sentence or inserted a single graphic in her proposal.

"How's the proposal coming?" she heard someone ask behind her. She turned to see her boss, Lorin.

"Uh…I…It's okay," she said. She could feel herself blush from the neck up.

Lorin walked into Jeagan's cubicle and perched on a low, beige file cabinet. "What's the matter, Jeagan?" Short and slightly bald, Lorin's dark eyes searched Jeagan's. "You're definitely not yourself lately, and you look like you haven't slept in a week."

Jeagan brushed away fresh, unwanted tears and looked up. "I'm sorry, Lorin. My head is just not in my work right now."

"I can see that," he said. "What's wrong? Anything I can do?"

"I wish you could." Unwilling to expose herself to more male ridicule, Jeagan added, "But, it's something personal."

"Do you need some time off to get things straightened out?"

Jeagan smiled. "That's probably a good idea. Could I take some time off after I get this proposal out the door?"

Lorin patted her shoulder. "Fine with me." He pushed himself to his feet. "Do you want me to get someone to finish up for you?"

"No." Jeagan shook her head. "I want to finish this myself, but I would like to take next week off."

"That works. But, I don't want to see you back here until you've got whatever it is sorted out."

* * *

With an effort, Jeagan pulled her thoughts back to the present. The horrible event that had brought her to Memphis could not be denied, and she could not run away from what she had come here to do.

Chapter Nine

Jeagan sat on the bed, opened the folder marked Furniture, and thumbed through the contents. There appeared to be hundreds of purchase orders in the folder as well as a thick list of in-house furniture at year-end, 1940. She pulled out the inventory list. Her heart pounded with fear of what she might find. As she thumbed through the inventory page by page, she found the pieces of furniture listed by room number. She flipped through the pages until room 807 appeared. The list itemized the furniture in the room at the end of 1940. The only desk listed was an antique-white writing desk, and the date of purchase was listed as 1930. Her desk was mahogany.

Okay. She sat back against the headboard. "What if…what if the desk was replaced sometime after 1940 but before 1944?" she said aloud. She reached into her handbag and pulled out a slip of paper with the number she had found on the bottom of the desk drawer. She flipped through the furniture list but found no item numbers listed. Disappointed, she continued to flip through the folder. Toward the back, she came across another type of list. This one contained furniture listed by category, room number, and stock numbers. It was dated January 01, 1943. Jeagan scanned the list until she came to the category of desks, then she moved her finger down the list until she came to room 807. The desk had an identification number: 010670.

Jeagan compared the number to the one written on the slip of paper, which was 018678. The numbers were not the same.

She laid the list aside and stood. Both numbers started with 01. The desk had to have come from the same furniture lot. Her heart raced. She needed to find out if she had copied the number correctly from her desk. She reached for the phone and dialed Caldwell & Ottonello in Denver.

"Lucie Larose. How can I help you?"

"Hi, Lucie. This is Jeagan. How're things going?"

"Hey, lady. What're you doing calling me? You're supposed to be on vacation," Lucie said.

"Look, Lucie, I need you to do me a favor," Jeagan said. "Can you go over to my condo on your lunch hour and check something for me? I hate to ask you to do it, but I really need your help."

"Sure, Jeag," Lucie said. "What do you want me to do?"

"I know this will sound weird, but I need for you to take a close look at the desk in my bedroom."

"Your desk?"

"I told you it would sound weird. I can't explain now, but this is important. I need for you to look under the desk on the bottom of the drawer and see if you can read the identification number and then call me from there. There's a spare key to my condo in the middle drawer of my desk there at the office." Jeagan thought she had written the number down correctly, but she had been pretty upset and maybe...

"Well...okay, but what's so urgent about a number on your desk?"

"Lucie, I'm sorry, but I can't explain right now. I just need to know what the number is."

"Okay, Jeag, but when you get back here, you owe me a drink...and an explanation."

"That's a promise. Oh, and another thing, don't actually sit at the desk."

"What?"

"Promise me you won't sit in the desk chair. I'll explain that later, too." Probably nothing would happen to Lucie, but Jeagan did not want to take any chances.

"Okay. Whatever you say," Lucie said.

Jeagan gave Lucie the direct number to her room at the hotel and then glanced at her watch again after she replaced the receiver. It was nearly twelve in Denver, so Lucie should leave the office shortly. Hopefully, she would call back within an hour.

Jeagan went to the window and pulled back the sheers. The streets were busy with traffic, as was the River beyond. If she

41

had possibly misread the number and it was really 010670, what next? She walked over to her mirror and looked at herself. The hotel registers would tell her if the Lloyd family had been guests at the hotel in the summer of 1944, but another trip to the basement would be risky. She wondered whether she really needed to do that.

"No," she said aloud. If the numbers matched, then a strong possibility existed that the rest of what she saw and heard was true. Jeagan shivered. If only she had never bought the desk and knew nothing about a fifty-year-old murder.

More than an hour later, the *brring* of the phone pierced the silence of Jeagan's room. She grabbed the receiver.

"Lucie?"

"Yep. It's me. I'm in your bedroom and I've found the number. It's pretty faded, but I think I can make it out."

"What is it?" Jeagan held her breath.

"Well, it looks like 018678."

Jeagan let out her breath. The numbers were not the same. Maybe she should go home and forget the whole thing.

"No, wait a minute," Lucie said. "Those are zeros not eights. It's 010670."

Chills raced up Jeagan's back and neck. "Are you sure?"

"That's what it looks like to me."

"Oh, my God!"

"Jeagan, are you all right? Tell me what's going on."

"Thanks for your help, Lucie, but I can't tell you right now. You're a real pal." Jeagan made an effort to lighten the conversation to put Lucie's mind at ease. "Can I bring you anything from Memphis?"

"Yeah, some warm weather. It's freezing here."

"It's gorgeous here. The trees are green and flowers are…"

"I don't want to hear it." Lucie laughed. "And don't come back all tanned either."

"I promise. And, Lucie, thanks. I owe you."

"You sure do and I intend to collect. By the way, are things any better between you and Brandon?"

"No, and that's another story I don't want to talk about right now. It's over between us. I gave him his ring back."

"Good move. I never thought he was good enough for you anyway. Well, guess I better get back to good ol' Caldwell & Ottonello. You got anything around here for lunch?"

"Probably not much, but help yourself to whatever you can find. And, thanks again."

"You're welcome. Call me if you need anything else. You'll be back when?"

"I'll be home on Saturday. Talk to you then."

Jeagan replaced the receiver. It was the same desk. Her hands trembled as she opened the Memphis telephone directory. She scanned the directory until she found the name "Lloyd," then searched under the "I's." There were three Isabels. How could there be so many and which, if any, was the right Isabel? And, maybe Isabel had married.

Jeagan scrawled the addresses on a slip of paper, grabbed her handbag, and headed for the door. She would find Isabel, if she was still alive, and she would have to look for her with the information she had.

Minutes later, Jeagan stepped out of the elevator and crossed the lobby to the concierge's desk. She asked for a map of the city and directions to the three addresses she had listed. The lobby was abuzz with what appeared to be a convention crowd. Suitcases and casually dressed men and women surrounded the front desk.

The concierge consulted the map after he glanced at the addresses on the list. "Let's see. This first address is in Frayser, about ten miles north of here. The next one's in Germantown, which is east of here. This last one is on Parkway, a straight shot down Union Avenue." The concierge circled the areas on the map where the streets were located. "This should help you."

"Thank you," Jeagan said. "Can you also help me with a rental car."

"Yes, ma'am. What kind would you like?"

Half an hour later, as Jeagan sat in a white Grand Am, she pulled out her map and decided to work from the farthest point back into the city. The first address was on Knox Road in Frayser. She checked the map and drove out Third Street to Highway 51 North. Forty-five minutes later, she found Knox Road—a narrow, paved road lined with fieldstone and brick houses set among graceful willows, budding mimosas, and towering cottonwoods. When she found the listed address, a neat fieldstone house, she parked on the street. Her intuition told her this was not the right house, but she might as well check to be sure.

"Kin I hep you?" a plump, elderly, black woman asked as she opened the door.

"Yes. I'm looking for Isabel Lloyd," Jeagan said.

"I'm Isabel Lloyd," the woman said guardedly.

"I'm looking for the Isabel Lloyd who stayed at the Peabody Hotel in the summer of 1944," Jeagan said, although she knew this was the wrong woman.

"Why, honey, I never even bin to the Peabody Hotel. Too rich for my blood." She grinned and showed a gold front tooth.

"Thank you anyway, Miss Lloyd. Sorry to have bothered you."

"That's aw right. I hope you find the right Is'bel."

Back in her car, Jeagan checked her map again. Germantown was east. She took Highway 51 back toward the city until it intercepted I-40, which circled back to the east. Once on I-40, she exited at Poplar Avenue and continued east. The homes became progressively plusher as she left the metropolitan area. After she turned off Poplar onto Germantown Road, she soon found Palmere Place. The address turned out to be a two-story colonial home. Jeagan parked, got out, and walked up the driveway.

A boy, who appeared to be about four years old, intercepted her before she reached the front door. "Hi," he said as he looked up at Jeagan. The light breeze ruffled his blond hair. "Who are

44

you?" He held two tiny race cars in one hand and wiped sand from his other hand onto his khaki shorts.

Jeagan bent forward. "My name is Jeagan. What's yours?"

"Mark and I'm going to be five next week," the boy said proudly.

Jeagan smiled. "That's great, Mark! Is your mother at home?"

"Sure. She's in the back yard."

"May I go back there and talk to her?"

"Uh." Mark hesitated. "I'm not s'posed to talk to strangers, but...I guess it's okay."

Jeagan was almost positive this was the wrong Isabel Lloyd also, but because she had come this far, she might as well talk with the boy's mother. She followed Mark up the driveway and around to the backyard.

"Mrs. Lloyd?" Jeagan said to the young, auburn-haired woman, who was on her hands and knees planting petunias in her flowerbed.

Startled, the woman looked up and pushed her hair out of her eyes with a gloved hand. "Yes, can I help you?" she said, as she stood and brushed dirt off her knees.

"Your son said it would be okay for me to come back."

Mrs. Lloyd gave her son a reprimanding look. "What can I do for you?" she asked Jeagan.

"I'm trying to find Isabel Lloyd. She would probably be in her seventies by now."

"I'm Isabel Lloyd, and as you can see, I've got a few more years before I reach seventy," the woman said.

"There's not an older Isabel Lloyd in your family, is there?"

"No. Lloyd is my husband's family's name, and I don't recall him ever mentioning another Isabel."

"That's what I was afraid of. Thank you anyway." Jeagan turned to leave and then turned back around. "Do you know any of the other Lloyds in Memphis that you're not related to by any chance?"

"No, I'm sorry. I don't."

Jeagan retraced her steps to the car. Once inside, she consulted her map again, and then headed back toward Poplar and the city. She was frustrated and hungry, so she searched for a place to grab a sandwich along the way. Familiar fast food places lined both sides of the street, but she decided against them. Soon, she saw a sign with a name she had heard somewhere before: Corky's. She pulled in the parking lot and entered the rustic restaurant with uneven wooden floors and walls of rough-hewn timber sprinkled with autographed pictures of celebrities. At least, she would get her fill of barbeque while she was in Memphis.

After she placed a take-out order, Jeagan waited impatiently for her sandwich. One more Isabel to go. "Please let her be the right one," Jeagan prayed.

Chapter Ten

While she ate her sandwich, Jeagan drove west on Poplar Avenue. She was not too far from Parkway, according to the map. When she reached Parkway, she turned left.

Soon she came to an imposing, white stucco, which appeared to be over a hundred years old, with a New Orleans-style wrought-iron balcony. Pink-blossomed azalea bushes bloomed beneath the front windows and white-blossomed azaleas lined the front walk. A massive magnolia tree, twin oaks, and several maples shaded the house and manicured grounds. This, she thought, looked like the kind of home where Isabel would live.

Jeagan pulled in the circular drive and parked near the front entrance. When she rang the doorbell, the door was soon opened by a tall, sixty-plus, black man, who was dressed in a dark suit and tie. For a moment, he stared at Jeagan, his eyes hard and cold.

Afraid the man would close the door in her face, Jeagan hurriedly asked if Isabel Lloyd lived at this address.

"Yes, she does," the man answered.

"Would it be possible for me to see her?" Jeagan asked.

"I'm afraid not," the man said, his voice deep and unfriendly. "She is not well and is resting."

"I see," Jeagan said. "Is there a time when I could come back and talk with her? It's very important."

"I don't think that would be possible. She's under a doctor's care and cannot have visitors," he said firmly.

"But...I wouldn't disturb her. I've come a long way to find her, and I would only take a few minutes of her time."

"I'm sorry, but you'll have to leave Miss." He started to close the door.

Jeagan put her hand against the door. "Please, I..."

"Who is it, Williams?" a stern voice asked from behind the butler.

"I don't know, Mrs. Harraway. She wants to see Miss Isabel, but I told her…"

"I'll handle this," the woman said.

The butler regarded Jeagan for a moment, then said, "Yes, ma'am." He opened the door.

Jeagan entered a spacious, white marble foyer. Twin staircases with wrought-iron balusters wound upward on either side of the hall and met in the middle of the second floor. An enormous crystal chandelier hung from the ceiling and a pale blue Persian carpet covered the central part of the foyer. A round, black marble table with wrought iron legs stood in the center of the carpet. On it stood a tall crystal vase filled with dozens of peach gladiolas.

"May I help you?" asked a tall, matronly woman, dressed in a dark brown suit. Her dark hair, liberally sprinkled with gray and pulled back severely from her pale face in a french twist, made her face look hard and brittle.

Somewhat intimidated by the woman's appearance, Jeagan momentarily lost her voice. "Yes. Uh…my name is Jeagan Christensen, and I'm trying to find Isabel Lloyd."

The woman smiled, but no warmth reached her eyes. "I'm Agnes Harraway, her sister. Maybe I can help you. Would you like to come into the living room? Maybe something to drink—coffee or lemonade?"

"I'd love some lemonade, thank you," Jeagan said, as she followed Agnes Harraway into the living room—alive with warm color. A celery-colored, overstuffed sofa faced two green-and-blue striped wingbacks over a cream-colored marble coffee table set on a blue Persian carpet similar to the one in the foyer. Polished cherrywood tables held painted, oriental lamps and silver-framed photographs of young, happy faces. Across the entrance hall, Jeagan could see a sleek, black, grand piano framed by French doors beyond. Plush, celery-colored carpet covered the floor. Polished cherrywood tables stood alongside green-and-blue floral armchairs and the same striped wingbacks.

The bright, sunlit rooms contrasted sharply with Agnes Harraway's appearance.

"Have a seat, won't you, Miss Christensen," Agnes said formally as she seated herself on a wingback. "Now, what business do you have with my sister?"

"Call me Jeagan," she said as she sank into the sofa. "I'm in town to do some research—for...for a possible magazine article. I recently bought a writing desk that originally came from the Peabody Hotel, and...and it piqued my curiosity about the time period it came from. Now, I'm interested in the year 1944, and...and especially the way people lived during the war years." She looked around nervously, making up her story as she went along. Again, she felt as if someone watched her. Out of the corner of her eye, she saw a shadow move away from the doorway that led into the foyer.

"How can my sister help you?" Agnes asked. She sat on the edge of the chair, her back ramrod straight.

As if on cue, the butler brought in a tray with lemonade for Jeagan and coffee for Agnes. He served their drinks.

"Thank you, Williams," Agnes said in a dismissive tone.

When she picked up her glass from the tray and sipped from it, Jeagan continued. "I would like to find out...uh, what the well-to-do people did to keep busy during the war: how the war affected their lives, what kinds of things they did for the war effort...that sort of thing."

"My sister couldn't possibly help you with that. She was only twenty in 1944."

Jeagan choked on her lemonade. Twenty would be the perfect age.

"Are you all right?" Agnes asked.

"I'm fine," Jeagan said. She set the glass on the tray and tried to recover her composure.

"Well," Agnes continued. "I was only nine then, so I couldn't help you either."

Jeagan tried another tactic. "Do you remember what your family did at that time for entertainment...say summer vacations."

"Let's see," Agnes said. She appeared to relax and enjoy the opportunity to reminisce. "Sometimes we drove down to New Orleans or to the Florida coast, but I think that summer—the summer of 1944—we stayed in Memphis. Yes, as I recall Isabel was not well that summer."

"Did your family possibly spend any time at the Peabody Hotel that summer?"

Agnes thought for a moment. "No, I'm sure we didn't."

Jeagan stood to leave. "I think I've wasted enough of your time, Mrs. Harraway. Do you think it might be possible for me to come back another time and talk to your sister for a few minutes? I'll be in town until Saturday, and I would really like to speak with her."

Agnes stood also. "I'll be glad to check with her when she awakens, and if she feels well enough, maybe she could see you tomorrow."

"I would really appreciate that. I'm at the Peabody. Please call me there if she feels well enough to see me."

Walking back to her rental car, Jeagan felt uneasy. Something was wrong. Agnes Harraway seemed almost too gracious, or was it merely the southern hospitality Jeagan had heard so much about? She looked back at the house, expecting to see— what she did not know.

Jeagan did not see the face that peered at her from behind the heavy drapery as she drove away.

*   *   *

Jeagan stopped in the lobby when she returned to the hotel. Along with the other tourists, she watched the ducks climb out of the fountain and then waddle across the lobby to the elevators. The sounds of clapping and laughter filled the lobby, which created a cheerful atmosphere. When the elevator doors closed behind the ducks, she chose a deep, leather club chair and sat down. The waitress from the lobby bar soon came over. Jeagan ordered a glass of asti. She watched the crowd disperse after the ducks departed. Some people stayed in the lobby and sat in scattered groups.

When her drink arrived, Jeagan sipped it and let the alcohol and the music calm her. She tried not to think and to relax for a few minutes. Her eyes wandered around the room. Various groups talked quietly in conversation areas around the lobby. Suddenly, she felt lonely and wished she had someone to talk to.

When she finished her wine, Jeagan returned to her room and ordered room service. She then sat in the chair by the window and watched the golden sun set over the Mississippi while she relived her conversation with Agnes Harraway. Possibly Agnes had told the truth and the Lloyd family had not spent any time that summer at the Peabody, but Isabel's age was right, and her family apparently was wealthy. What if Agnes had lied? There could be no real reason for her to lie, Jeagan thought. Agnes had no way of knowing Jeagan's motive for asking questions about what their family did in the summer of 1944.

Skirt the issue, she could, but the fact remained that another trip to the basement was necessary, much as she hated the idea. There was no way around it. The identification numbers on her desk proved that she was on the right track, and she had to know if Isabel and her family were in the hotel in July of 1944.

When her meal arrived, Jeagan forced down a few bites of the clam chowder and a dinner salad. She placed the tray in the hall and then pulled a dark sweater over her shirt, stuffed the folder inside, and left her room.

Two men stood at the elevator when she arrived. One of them glanced her way, gave her the once over, and smiled. Jeagan returned the smile but ignored the men. When the elevator arrived, the men stood aside to allow Jeagan to enter first. She smiled and nodded. The men continued their conversation, about the inexpensive price of real estate in

Memphis compared to California, until the elevator stopped in the lobby.

Jeagan stood to the side of the elevator doors while the men exited so she could not be seen from the lobby. No one entered in the lobby and momentarily the doors closed. The elevator continued to the basement. When the doors opened again, she held them, stuck her head out, and looked both ways. The basement hallway appeared to be empty. She stepped out and let the doors close behind her. Quickly, she made her way down the stairs to the sub-basement.

When she arrived at the records room door, she found that it was still unlocked. Quietly, she opened it, stepped inside, and closed the door behind her. She searched for the light switch and turned the lights on. This time, she laid her sweater on the floor and stuffed it against the door to fill the void so no light would escape.

First, Jeagan returned the furniture folder to its place in the file cabinet and then began to search for hotel registers. She searched through the first file cabinet in the row marked 1940 but found no registers. The second cabinet held only used receipt books. Maybe, she thought, the registers were kept in another location, but she continued her search. When she reached the fourth cabinet in the row, she heard voices in the hall. She ran to the door, turned off the light, grabbed her sweater, and backed against the wall behind the door. In pitch-black darkness, she heard the knob turn and slowly the door opened, which allowed the dim light from the hall into the room. Someone took a step inside, flipped on the light, and opened the door a few more inches.

Jeagan's heart pounded in her chest. Surely, whoever it was in the doorway could hear it.

The next moment, the lights went out and the door closed. A key ground in the lock. Jeagan's stomach lurched. She had not been caught, but someone had locked her inside. "Please let there be a way to unlock the door," she prayed. She stayed where she was for a full five minutes before moving. After her heart rate slowed and she was sure the hallway outside was quiet, she got down on her hands and knees and restuffed the sweater into the space between the door and the floor. She stood and groped for the light switch when no more light from the hallway could be seen. The light on, she checked to see if the door could be unlocked from the inside.

The lock clicked as she turned the door handle. Relieved, she relocked the door from the inside and resumed her search where she had left off and methodically made her way down the row. With only two cabinets left, she came across a drawer of black, bound volumes. These had to be the guest registers! She pulled one out and opened it.

"Yes!" The date on the guest register was 1940. After she replaced it, she opened the next drawer. Volumes for 1941. Three drawers down should be 1944. She opened that drawer and pulled out a volume—February 1944. Where was July? Ten volumes back, she found July and scanned the pages for the Lloyd name. What was Isabel's father's name? She had no idea. It was too late to worry about that now. If she got lucky and found any Lloyd in room 807, she would remember his name and then see if she could find out Isabel's father's name later.

She chose the volume that began with July first. On the second day of July, there was an entry, "Mr. Lucius Lloyd." No "Mrs." was listed and the room number was 302. She scanned the page. On July third, there was an entry for a "Mr. and Mrs. Tyler Lloyd," but the room number was wrong. She flipped to the next page. The next Lloyd appeared on July fourth. The name was "Mr. and Mrs. Robert Lloyd." She ran her finger across the page. The room number was 807! This had to be Isabel's parents. Agnes had lied.

Jeagan replaced the volume with shaking hands and headed for the door. She turned off the light, listened for any noise in the hall, and retrieved her sweater from the floor. Dust covered it. Without thinking, she shook it.

"*Achoo!*" She held her breath and listened. All was quiet in the hall. Hopefully, no one had heard her. After a few minutes, she groped for the door handle in the dark and turned the lock. The door creaked slightly as it opened. Jeagan looked both ways down the hall. At one end of the hall, she saw a man bent over a bucket with his back to her. She moved into the hall, silently closed the door behind her, and hurried toward the stairs.

Voices came from the stairwell. She stopped in her tracks. Her breath caught in her throat. She looked around and tried the door nearest her, found it unlocked and ducked inside. Questions about her presence in the basement were not what she had in mind, especially since she was not a good liar. Moments later, she heard two women talking as they opened the door from the stairway and walked past her door. The hallway was soon quiet again. Jeagan opened the door and peeked down the hallway. The two women were at the other end of the hall. She dashed for the stairwell, quietly opened the door, and ran up to the basement level. No one appeared to be in the hall there when she opened the stairwell door. Nonchalantly, she walked over to the elevator and pressed the up button. The elevator doors opened momentarily. Once inside, she punched the button for the tenth floor, then shuddered involuntarily and sank back against the wall.

She hoped the elevator would not stop on the first floor. It did not; the next stop was the tenth floor. As the door opened, she looked down the hall. One man walked toward her. He stopped at the room next to hers, fumbled in his pocket for his room key, and dropped it as Jeagan reached her room.

"Why, hello there." The man, heavy-set with a ruddy complexion, let his eyes run up and down Jeagan's body.

Jeagan nodded briefly before she disappeared into her room.

* * *

When he heard the stairway door close behind Jeagan, the sandy-haired man, who was bent over the bucket, straightened. He turned to follow her but ran into two Asian women.

The women eyed the tall, tanned man—dressed in khakis and a red golf shirt— apparently suspicious of strangers on the lower level.

"Excuse me," he said, smiling. "I seem to be lost. Is the workout room on this level?"

He could see the women visibly relax, obviously used to lost guests.

"Exercise room on nex' level." The younger of the women pointed down the hall. "Take stair."

The man thanked the women and headed toward the stairs. When he could no longer hear the women, he pulled out his cell phone. "Our friend spent some time in the records storage area of the hotel. She had something inside her sweater when she went in, but I don't know if it was still there when she came out."

"Any idea what it was?" came the response from the person on the other end of the line.

"Not yet, but I'll find out."

* * *

Jeagan stripped off her clothes and stepped into the shower. Hot water ran over her body. She washed off the fear and tension that had built all day, shampooed her hair vigorously and stood in the shower until she felt warm and relaxed. After towelling her hair and body, she slipped on the terry-cloth robe provided by the hotel and sat in front of the mirror in the bedroom to comb out her hair.

She had the proof she needed that Isabel's family had been in the hotel in room 807, but the information would be useless unless she could get in to see Isabel. She wondered whether Agnes Harraway would keep her word and arrange for her to see her sister. Agnes had lied about staying at the Peabody in 1944. But why? Possiby, Jeagan thought, Agnes did not remember staying at the Peabody Hotel the summer she was nine years old.

Jeagan began to yawn, her body unwinding and dead tired. She dried her hair, checked to make sure she had locked the door, and then crawled into bed. There had to be a way for her to get in to see Isabel, but she would worry about that tomorrow.

Chapter Eleven

In the morning, Jeagan awoke later than usual. When she looked in the mirror, she noticed puffy, dark circles under her eyes. It is true that crime does not pay, she thought. She brushed out her hair and dressed in tiny black-and-white checked slacks, a white-cotton pullover sweater, and black flats. She went downstairs and hoped that by the time she finished breakfast, she would have a call from Agnes Harraway. The coffee shop was full when she arrived. The hostess told her it would be at least a fifteen-minute wait. Jeagan gave her name and turned to sit in the waiting area.

"You can join me," someone said from a nearby table.

Jeagan turned around to see an attractive black man, who sat alone at a table for two. He was dressed in a gray, pin-striped suit and held a copy of the *Wall Street Journal* over his coffee and English muffin.

Jeagan smiled. "Thanks, but I wouldn't want to impose."

The man stood. Jeagan noted that he must be around thirty, slightly over six feet tall with broad shoulders and a trim waist. A weight lifter, she thought

"No imposition at all," the man said. "I'd welcome the company. Besides, I don't really like to eat alone."

Jeagan hesitated only a moment. She also hated to eat alone. After a nod to the hostess, she walked over to the table.

The man extended his hand. "I'm Darrell Hannah."

Jeagan sat down and tried not to laugh. "Daryl Hannah?"

He grinned. "I know, it's funny. You can call me Madison. A lot of people do since the movie *Splash*."

Jeagan laughed again and reached out to shake hands with the man. "I'm Jeagan Christensen. It's nice to meet you, Madison."

Madison sat down and folded his paper. "Are you a guest at the hotel?"

She nodded and opened the menu. "I've been here since Monday."

A waitress stopped at the table. "Would you like some coffee?"

"Please," Jeagan said.

"A refill for you, sir?" the waitress asked.

Madison held out his cup. "Yes, thank you." He turned back toward Jeagan. "Are you in town on business?" He poured cream into his coffee.

"Sort of. Uh…I'm here to do research on antiques. I'm actually a technical writer. I work for an engineering firm in Denver."

"Denver? I haven't been there in years," Madison said. "I'd love to get back there sometime and spend a few days on the slopes." He thought for a moment. "I believe the place we skied when I was in law school was Copper Mountain."

"That's one of my favorites," Jeagan said. "So, you're an attorney?"

He nodded. "Afraid so. I'm at Atwell and Frazier on Front Street."

"What kind of law do you practice?" Jeagan sipped her coffee and enjoyed the strong chicory taste.

"Corporate stuff—pretty dull most of the time." He glanced at his watch. "In fact, I have an appointment with an out-of-town client in the lobby in fifteen minutes to deliver some papers for his signature."

The waitress approached the table. "Are you ready to order?"

"Yes," Jeagan said. "Give me a second." She scanned the menu. "I'll have a Denver omelette."

Madison laughed.

Jeagan grinned. "No, make that eggs benedict." When the waitress left, she said. "Old habits and all that."

"How long will you be in town?" Madison asked.

"I'm not sure, probably only a few more days. I've got to be back at work on Monday."

"How about having dinner with me one night before you go? I could show you Beale Street. There's some good food down there and great blues bands."

Jeagan hesitated. Madison seems like a genuinely nice person—and he's an attorney, she thought. What harm would it do to meet him on Beale Street and have dinner with him?

"Okay," Jeagan said. "That sounds like fun."

"How about Friday? I've got court in the afternoon. I could meet you here in the lobby, say around five, and we could just walk over."

"That's fine." Jeagan smiled.

"Well, I guess I'd better go. Don't want to keep the client waiting." Madison laid his briefcase on the table, opened it, and dropped the *Journal* inside. "Oh, I hate to leave you to eat by yourself," he added, as the waitress arrived with Jeagan's order.

Jeagan smiled. "Don't worry. I don't mind. You don't want to be late for your appointment."

Madison checked his watch again and stood. "No, I don't." He studied Jeagan's face for a moment. "Nice talking with you, and I look forward to seeing you on Friday."

"Me, too," Jeagan said.

Jeagan ate her breakfast leisurely, since she could do nothing but wait. She checked the time. Ten-thirty. If she didn't hear from Agnes Harraway by eleven, she would call her. After breakfast, she headed back to her room. She looked to see if Madison was still in the lobby as she passed through. He was. He sat with two other men, their heads bent over documents spread on a table between them.

Madison glanced up and saw Jeagan. He smiled.

Jeagan waved and turned toward the elevators. Might be a good idea to know a local attorney while I'm in town, she thought.

Back in her room, she paced the floor. "Ring phone!" Finally, at eleven, she could not stand it any longer. She opened the telephone directory, found the listing for Isabel Lloyd on Parkway, and wondered why the listing was in Isabel's name instead of Agnes'. It appeared Agnes must have moved in with Isabel at some point—maybe to take care of her.

Jeagan dialed the number.

"The Lloyd residence," a female voice answered. Jeagan had expected the butler to answer.

"Could I speak with Isabel Lloyd, please?" Jeagan asked and prayed she could get through.

"May I tell her who's calling?"

"My name is Jeagan Christensen. Tell her it's very important."

"Just a minute, please. I'll see if Miz Isabel can come to the phone."

Jeagan waited anxiously. She could not believe her luck. Soon, someone picked up another extension.

"Hello?" a soft, clear voice said.

"Miss Isabel Lloyd?"

"Yes. May I help you?"

"Uh…uh," Jeagan stammered, then the words tumbled out. "My name is Jeagan Christensen. I've travelled eleven hundred miles from Denver to see you about a very important matter."

"What matter is that?" the soft voice asked.

"Well, it's about the events that happened in 1944 while you and your family were guests at the Peabody Hotel."

"What did you say?" the voice rose in alarm.

"It's urgent that I see you. I'm staying at the Peabody—"

Click. The phone was disconnected at the other end.

Jeagan held the phone out and looked at it, then placed it to her ear again. She could not believe the woman had hung up on her.

Discouraged, Jeagan replaced the phone. There had to be a way to get Isabel to talk to her. The question was how? Jeagan needed proof that Alan had been murdered, or had at least disappeared, if there really was an Alan McCarter. But, Alan had to be real. Everything else had checked out so far.

If Alan was real and had disappeared, it would have been in the papers, wouldn't it? Absolutely! She opened the phone

60

directory and soon found what she needed—the local newspaper office. The address appeared to be only a short distance down Union Avenue. She grabbed her handbag and headed to the lobby. First, she stopped in one of the gift shops to buy a writing pad, then retrieved her rental car, and drove east on Union Avenue.

*   *   *

Jeagan arrived at the newspaper office—spacious and open with award-winning articles framed and displayed on the sunny walls—ten minutes later. She checked with a helpful, middle-aged woman with a cheerful smile at the information desk and was directed to the Morgue.

"I'd like to see the newspapers for the summer of 1944," Jeagan said to the clerk when she arrived in the newspaper's Morgue.

"Those would be on microfiche," the gray-haired clerk said. He indicated rows of file cabinets and microfiche readers at the back of the room.

"Could you show me how to use the microfiche reader?" Jeagan said.

"Sure."

Jeagan watched as the clerk pulled microfiche from a file cabinet and loaded it into the reader. Soon, she scanned news articles from the forties. She noticed a picture of women in baggy pants with their hair wrapped in headscarves at a Boeing plant in Seattle. The women were driving rivets into airplanes. The picture brought back memories of the stories her grandmother used to tell her about the war days and how the women handled the jobs normally done by the men.

The papers through July fourteenth related accounts of the war in the Pacific and in Europe, but made no mention of Alan McCarter. She continued to scan. Nothing about Alan McCarter appeared in the rest of July.

She scanned the August newspapers until her attention was caught by an article in the society section on August tenth. It read: "Miss Isabel Lloyd, daughter of Mr. and Mrs. Robert Lloyd of Memphis, has announced her plans to travel to Switzerland to study piano for a year at the Shubert Institute of Music. Already an accomplished pianist, Miss Lloyd will study under the direction of Herr Franz Leipzig."

"I was right," Jeagan whispered to herself. Her pulse quickened. The article confirmed that Isabel's father's name was Robert. And, it appeared he had hustled Isabel out of town after he killed her fiancé.

After a scan through the rest of August, Jeagan found nothing else about Isabel, but when Jeagan reached August twenty-eighth, she found an article on a back page about Alan.

The article read: "Alan McCarter, son of Mr. and Mrs. Franklin McCarter of Merle, Arkansas, has been officially listed Away Without Official Leave from the United States Navy. McCarter failed to report back to his unit on July 14th. Franklin McCarter stated he has not seen his son since the morning of July 13th, when he left Merle for Memphis to visit with a friend before he reported back to the Naval Air Station in Millington. Ruth McCarter, Alan's mother, added that her son had spent a lot of his leave in Memphis, and, although he had not admitted as much, she suspected he was involved with a woman there. The family asks that anyone with information about Alan's disappearance please contact them at Rt. 6, Box 23 in Merle."

Jeagan shuddered as she read the article. Now, more than ever, she had to get to Isabel and tell her what really happened to Alan, if she did not already know. For some reason, Jeagan strongly suspected that she did not.

Jeagan thanked the clerk and drove back to the Peabody. She parked her car in the hotel garage and then, because of a need to relieve her frustration, walked toward Mid-America Mall. Soon she came on a park. Through the trees, she saw a fountain.

"Oh, my God!" She walked over to the fountain. It was the one she had seen in the last flashback. Her eyes scanned the park for the white gazebo. It was still there. She grabbed the back of a bench to steady herself and then slid onto it. This was where the murder had happened in 1944. Suddenly, she could not breathe. She needed to get away from the park. Her heart raced as she jumped up and ran along the path that led to Second Street. Suddenly, she collided with a man who stood with his back to her.

"I'm sorry," she said and looked up at a tall, sandy-haired man.

The man turned toward Jeagan. "That's okay." A frown creased his forehead. "Are you all right?"

Jeagan felt like she was going to be sick. "I'm...I'm."

"Here, let me help you." The man took her by the arm.

"Let go of me!" Jeagan jerked her arm away. She raced out of the park and along Second Street toward the hotel. When she reached the Peabody, gasping for air, she stopped to look behind her, but did not see the man. She entered the hotel and took the elevator to her room.

Once inside, she sat on the bed and tried to stop shaking. Had the man tried to abduct her or had he tried to help her? Upset as she was at seeing the actual murder scene and being grabbed by the man, she felt sick at her stomach and could not think clearly. She went into the bathroom, soaked a wash cloth in cold water and pressed it to her face and throat until the queasiness passed. When she returned to the bedroom, she noticed the red light on the phone. She grabbed the receiver and called the front desk.

"May I help you?" the hotel operator said.

"This is Jeagan Christensen. Do I have a message?"

"Yes. A Miss Isabel Lloyd called at eleven-thirty. She left a message for you. She asked that you meet her at four o'clock tomorrow afternoon at the Orpheum Theatre."

"Thank you." Incredulous, Jeagan replaced the receiver. "I don't believe it." She fell backward onto the bed. Now that she had an appointment with Isabel Lloyd, she had to actually tell her what may have happened to Alan McCarter. What if Alan had reappeared somewhere between August 1944 and the present? If so, Isabel would think Jeagan was a nut-house escapee.

Chapter Twelve

Jeagan sat up on the bed and reached for the phone directory on the nightstand. She thumbed through the first few pages of the book until she found the list of area codes. When she spotted the area code for Arkansas, she dialed information and asked for a listing for Alan McCarter. There was no listing. Is it possible one of Alan's parents could still be alive, she wondered? She asked the operator for a listing for Franklin McCarter. Moments later, she had a telephone number for Franklin McCarter in Merle, Arkansas.

Should she call Alan's parents? They had to be in their nineties by now—if both of them were still alive. Maybe they would not talk to her, a stranger, if she called and asked questions about their son, especially if he has been dead since 1944, Jeagan thought. Maybe it would be better if she drove to Merle. She might not have to bother the family after all. If the town was still a farm community, as Isabel's father had implied in their confrontation in 1944, then Jeagan might be able to find out what she needed to know from any of the local people. She grabbed her handbag and keys and left the room.

In the lobby, Jeagan approached the concierge's desk and asked for a map of Arkansas.

"Is there any particular place you're interested in?" the fortyish, blonde concierge asked as she opened a map of Arkansas and spread it on her desk.

"I need to find Merle. How far is it from here?"

"Not very." The concierge consulted the map. She took a yellow marker from her desk and highlighted the highway Jeagan should take.

*   *   *

Once on the Interstate, Jeagan enjoyed the drive. The scenery took her mind off her problems for a while. She crossed the Mississippi River on the Memphis-Arkansas bridge and entered West Memphis, Arkansas—a riverfront town. The town was small but alive with activity. She stopped at a traffic light by a dog-racing track where she heard the announcer yell, "Here comes Rusty!" over the loud speaker. As she continued through town, she noted that the truck stops were full of eighteen wheelers. If old sayings were true, there must be good food in this town, since truckers knew where to find it.

After she passed through West Memphis, Jeagan noticed several housing developments and then suddenly the suburbs stopped and the farming communities started. Freshly plowed fields ran along both sides of the highway. Jeagan wondered if they still grew cotton in the area.

Soon, she came into the town of Merle, Arkansas, population 1345. She drove down the main street that consisted of a hardware store, a feed store, a gas station, a restaurant, a grocery store, and a dry goods store. She chose the feed store—a red, wooden building with the name Hadley's Feed Store painted across the arched façade in giant white letters. It seemed the likely place to find out about the people who lived here.

Several men, dressed in jeans and various colors of cotton shirts, turned to openly stare at her when she entered. She felt out of place, but walked across the rough, wooden floor, approached the counter, and put on her friendliest smile. "I'm trying to find the McCarter family. I wonder if someone can tell me where they live."

"Which McCarter—Jeremiah, Adam, or Franklin?" a heavy, burly man asked. He leaned against the red formica counter. Jeagan noted that he wore overalls and a Razorbacks baseball cap, but no welcoming smile. His brown eyes narrowed and focused on Jeagan from beneath the bill of his cap. He placed the feed and seed catalog he had been reading on the counter.

"Franklin." Jeagan noticed that the man did not mention the name Alan.

"What do you want with old man McCarter?" A look of suspicion crossed the man's face. No one else spoke. They stared at Jeagan, their expressions blank.

"I'd like to ask him a few questions about his son."

"Franklin's getting on in years," the proprietor of the store said—tall, leathery, and neatly dressed in jeans and a yellow golf shirt. "If you need to talk to him about one of his sons, maybe you should go see the son in person."

"How many sons does he have?" Jeagan turned to the proprietor.

"Three. Jeremiah, Adam, and Trenton."

"What about Alan?"

The reaction was immediate. Several of the men actually gasped. One started to cough.

The proprietor stared at Jeagan, his eyes hard. "What about Alan?"

"That's what I'm here to find out," Jeagan said.

"What do you want to know about him?" the proprietor asked, his voice hard.

Jeagan asked. "Does he live around here?"

The proprietor shook his head. "No."

"Do you know where he lives?"

"No." He offered no information.

Somewhat annoyed, Jeagan said, "Well, will you tell me where his father lives?" Jeagan wished she had written down the address from the article in the newspaper.

The proprietor looked down at the counter, as if unsure of what to say. "Why do you want to know about Alan?"

"I'm working on a research project and…"

"I don't think it would be a good idea to bother Frank. He's an old man—nearly cripple. Bringing up bad memories can only hurt him."

"I'm not here to hurt him. I'm here to help him." Jeagan was now almost sure that Alan was dead, but she needed to talk to his father to find out if Alan had been seen after July of 1944.

The proprietor of the store folded his arms across his chest. "I think you had better leave now."

Jeagan retreated to her car. "I thought southerners were supposed to be friendly," she said aloud still feeling the coldness in the stare of the man behind the counter and the other men in the store. She drove to a service station on the corner where she found a phone booth. She flipped through the pages until she came to Franklin McCarter, Route 6, Box 23. A few minutes later, Jeagan was back in her car and on her way to Route 6, thanks to a helpful service station attendant.

The McCarter home, when Jeagan found it fifteen minutes later, was a small, white clapboard house, badly in need of paint. The front porch contained a faded floral couch and two metal chairs with flaky green paint. When Jeagan pulled into the grassless yard, she was greeted by two dogs, which appeared out of nowhere. Both were thin, brown-and-white mixed breeds. They greeted Jeagan as if she were a long, lost friend by jumping on the car door and wagging their tails. Jeagan opened the door and stepped into the yard, only to have the dogs jump on her and lick her hands.

"At least somebody's friendly in this town," she said, as she patted first one dog's head and then the other. When she looked up, she saw an elderly man on the porch. He said nothing but squinted at Jeagan with faded blue eyes out of a tanned, furrowed face. His short, gray hair stuck out from under a red cap. His tall, stooped, frame appeared lost in a plaid shirt and faded jeans.

"Mr. McCarter?" Jeagan asked, tentatively.

"That's right." The man neither smiled nor frowned. "What can I do for you?"

Jeagan approached the porch. "I'd like to talk to you."

McCarter continued to stare at Jeagan.

"It's about your son…Alan." Jeagan stopped at the edge of the porch and watched Alan's father closely for a reaction.

Shock showed in McCarter's eyes momentarily, then his expression closed. "Alan's dead," he said, no emotion evident in his voice.

Gooseflesh crept across Jeagan's back and down her arms. "I thought as much, Mr. McCarter. What I would like to talk to you about is when Alan died." She stood her ground at the foot of the steps.

McCarter stuffed his hands in his pockets and said, "1944."

Tears formed in Jeagan's eyes. "Mr. McCarter, I hate to ask you this question, but do you know how your son died? Did he die of an illness?"

McCarter pulled his hands out of his pockets and pulled his cap off his head and pushed his hair back and replaced his cap. "I don't know. What do you really want, young lady?" A look of suspicion and hurt filled his eyes.

"You probably won't believe this, but I think I know how your son died."

Unshed tears shone in McCarter's eyes. "How could anybody as young as you know anything about my son? He died before you were born."

"Yes, sir. I know that, but I think I've been allowed to see what happened to him, and maybe I can help you bury your son at last."

"I don't know what you're talking about, but if you know anything about Alan, you better come up on the porch and sit down."

"Thank you, Mr. McCarter." Jeagan climbed the steps and sat on one of the metal chairs.

McCarter limped over to the faded couch and sat down. Although his manner was passive, his eyes showed his anxiety.

Jeagan began her story slowly and calmly. She told McCarter how she had bought the antique desk and worked her way up to the murder she had witnessed.

McCarter remained silent throughout the tale, his face expressionless, his eyes focused on his fields.

When she came to the actual murder, Jeagan hesitated, not wanting to hurt Alan's father. "I'm sorry to have to tell you this, but I saw Isabel's father shoot your son."

McCarter sat still for a few moments and then turned toward Jeagan. "Young lady, either the Almighty favored you with some kinda second sight or you're crazy. I'm inclined toward crazy." McCarter rose from his chair, walked into his house, and closed the door.

Stunned, Jeagan walked slowly back to her car, followed by the two overly friendly dogs. Tears stung her eyes as she opened the car door. I only meant to help, she thought, but guilt tugged at her subconscious. Who did she want to help, herself or Franklin McCarter? If she had not needed verification of Alan's disappearance and probable death, would she have come to Merle, Arkansas to seek out his family? "Yes, I would," she said aloud.

The dogs sat down beside her car. She patted each one again before she got in. Dust flew in her open window as she pulled out of the yard and drove down the gravel road away from Franklin McCarter's farm. When she glanced in the rearview mirror, she noticed a brown Taurus parked a half-mile down the road under a tree. The driver resembled the man she had seen in Court Square earlier, but from this distance, she could not be sure. She watched in the mirror to see if he pulled out to follow her. The car was still there when she turned at a fork in the road, so she ignored the incident.

*   *   *

After she arrived back at the Peabody an hour and a half later, Jeagan stopped in the lobby for a glass of wine and to regroup her thoughts. She sat in an overstuffed armchair close to the fountain and let the soothing sound of the water take her mind off Franklin McCarter. While she waited for her drink, she leaned back in the chair and closed her eyes. She opened her eyes a few minutes later to find a man standing in front of her.

70

Startled, she jumped and straightened in her chair. The man—middle-aged and pudgy with dark hair graying at the temples—seemed vaguely familiar. His dark green eyes sparkled with life from his round, slightly florid face.

"Didn't mean to startle you. I saw you sittin' here all by yourself, and I wondered if you'd like some company," the man said.

"Thank you, but no. I've had a rough day, and I need to relax for a minute," Jeagan said, trying to be polite.

Uninvited, the man sat in a chair across an end table from Jeagan and deposited his drink on the table. "What you need is cheering up," he said with a grin. "You look like you've lost your last friend."

Jeagan could not resist the man's cheerful manner. "Maybe I could use a good laugh. I haven't had many of those lately."

"That's more like it." The man extended his hand to Jeagan. "I'm Edward Coffey. Sell life insurance, annuities, that sort of thing."

"Hello, Edward. I'm Jeagan Christensen. I nose into other people's business." Jeagan smiled. Her face relaxed somewhat.

Edward's eyebrows rose. "So, you're a private detective?"

"Not exactly. This is personal research." Realization dawned in Jeagan's eyes. "Say, aren't you in the room next to mine?"

"That's right. I've seen you around for the last few days and thought you might need a little company." Jeagan detected a definite leer in Edward's eyes.

"I'm actually pretty busy." She turned as the waitress approached and set her glass of wine on the table. Jeagan signed the ticket, thanked the waitress and turned to Edward.

"What are you doing in Memphis?" Jeagan asked out of politeness, not interest.

Edward took a long drink of what smelled to Jeagan like bourbon. "I'm here for a conference at the Convention Center. It doesn't start until tomorrow, but I came early to visit our branch office and train some newly hired folks."

"That's nice," Jeagan said.

"Hey. If you're not busy, how about having dinner with me? My treat." His puppy-dog eyes pleaded for her to answer yes.

Jeagan half expected Edward to pant or drool any minute. "No, but thank you anyway. I'm going to finish my drink and then go back to my room and order room service." She sipped her wine and sat back in the chair. The lamp on the table blocked Edward from her view.

"Okay. I can take a hint. You'd rather be alone." Edward took his glass from the table. He rose from his chair and smiled at Jeagan. "If you change your mind, I'll be over there in the Dux Restaurant."

"Thanks, Edward, but like I said, I'm going back to my room soon and I'll be in for the night."

When she finished her drink, Jeagan opened her handbag to find her room key. The handbag felt lighter than usual. She looked inside and realized her billfold was gone. Immediately she thought of Edward. How could he have taken it when my handbag was on the floor beside me, she wondered? Then she realized she had her eyes closed when Edward first approached her chair. Not wanting to accuse anyone, she decided to check her car before she took any action. She remembered that she had her billfold last at a service station in West Memphis.

Jeagan left the hotel through the rear door of the lobby. Several minutes passed before she located her car in the four-story garage. Through the window, she saw her billfold on the passenger seat. She laughed and shook her head. Wouldn't she have looked like an idiot if she had gone into Dux and accused Edward Coffey of stealing her billfold? That would be like the pot calling the kettle black, as her mother used to say. She opened the car door and reached across the driver's seat for the billfold. As she did, she saw a brown Taurus pull into the lot. She ducked down into the seat when she recognized the man. It was the sandy-haired man she had seen at the park and again in Merle, Arkansas. When he passed her and entered the ramp to the second floor of the garage, she locked her car and hurried into the hotel. She stopped by the front desk to ask for the security guard. The desk clerk was busy with another guest when she approached.

After several minutes, Jeagan changed her mind. Maybe she was mistaken. Maybe the man was not the same man she had seen in Arkansas. There must be a million brown Tauruses out on the road and hundreds of men with sandy-blond hair. Jeagan turned and crossed the lobby to the elevators.

* * *

As he watched the elevator doors close, the man pulled out his cell phone. He dialed a number and waited. When the party on the other end answered, he said, "I followed her to Arkansas today. She visited Franklin McCarter."

Chapter Thirteen

Locked safely inside her room, Jeagan turned on the television for distraction. Her mind overflowed with thoughts and impressions, but she wanted to give herself some time before she faced the real truth of the things she had discovered.

Dinner seemed like a good idea. She opened the room service menu and scanned it. Lamb with potatoes au gratin and a Greek salad sounded good. The order placed, she walked over to the window and gazed out at the pink clouds that strayed across the lavender evening sky.

She leaned against the windowframe and longed for someone to talk to. For the thousandth time, she wished her mom were still alive. Jeagan remembered the many times she had gone crying to her mom for one reason or another—grades, boys, disappointments. Her mom always stopped whatever she was doing and gave Jeagan her undivided attention. Always, she took Jeagan's problems seriously, and somehow the problems seemed less serious after they were shared.

A fond memory for Jeagan, she recalled the floral placemats on her mom's glass-topped kitchen table. Often Jeagan sat at the antiqued-white rattan table with the green chairs and watched her mother make hot chocolate in winter or iced tea in summer. All the while, her mother listened as Jeagan poured her heart out. Never once did her mother interrupt or imply that Jeagan's problems were unimportant. Why couldn't her dad or Brandon do that, Jeagan wondered. Why did all the men in her life seem to dismiss her problems and concerns as inconsequential?

The light knock on the door startled Jeagan out of her reverie. She jumped and grabbed her heart. "Who is it?" she called out as she crossed to the door.

"Room service," said a voice from the hallway.

Relieved, Jeagan opened the door for the waiter, who wheeled in a cart with her dinner. Jeagan thanked the waiter and tipped him. When he opened the door to leave, Jeagan held the door for him. She spotted Edward Coffey walking along the hall toward her. He waved and grinned and then quickened his step. Before he could reach her room, Jeagan waved and closed the door. A little of that man went a long way. In fact, between Edward and the man with the sandy-blond hair, Jeagan almost felt like a prisoner in her room.

She picked at her dinner, not really hungry. Seated in front of the windows opened on the city, Jeagan considered all that had happened since she arrived in Memphis. Every bit of information she had collected seemed to confirm that the flashbacks she had had were actual events. Hopefully, her talk with Isabel tomorrow would be the final piece to confirm everything except the actual murder.

Jeagan wondered what Isabel must be thinking at this moment. After she had hung up on Jeagan, why had Isabel called to arrange a meeting? Obviously, Jeagan had touched a nerve of some sort. She could only hope that her meeting with Isabel would go better than the one with Franklin McCarter.

Still feeling guilty about McCarter's reaction to her visit, she again wondered if she had been wrong to visit him. His pain was obvious. But, their conversation confirmed that the murder she had somehow witnessed in all likelihood had taken place. Wouldn't McCarter want to know what happened to Alan? If he somehow decided to believe Jeagan, then he would at least have closure. She could not bring herself to regret that he would have that.

When she ate all she could, Jeagan opened the door to set the tray in the hall. The door to the next room opened—Coffey's room. She jumped back into her room and pushed the door shut. He called her name, but she chose to ignore him. The man was a pest. Jeagan could not wait to meet with Isabel and get out of this town.

She padded barefoot across to the bed and sat down. If she got out of Memphis on Saturday as planned, what would she do on the weekend? It would be her first weekend alone without Brandon. Maybe she would go skiing at Copper Mountain. At the thought, her spirits lightened. Lucie would probably go with her. She was generally free and ready to ski on most weekends now that her fiancé was on a six-month assignment in Alaska.

The question now was what would she do with her time until four o'clock tomorrow afternoon. She spotted a brochure on the table by the window that listed the sights in Memphis. The first one showed a picture of Graceland, Home of the King. Jeagan smiled to herself. She enjoyed Elvis' music but thought she would pass on a visit to his former home and shrine. As she read the brochure, her attention was drawn to pictures of Mudd Island—an island connected to Memphis by a tram. It appeared the island contained a museum of Mississippi River history, restaurants, and a scaled replica of the River from its origin in Minnesota to where it emptied into the Gulf of Mexico. Now, that might be interesting and it would take her mind off Isabel.

Later, as Jeagan lay in bed unable to sleep, she realized what a mess she had gotten herself into. She had hurt one person today and tomorrow would hurt another. Maybe she should have taken her dad's advice and kept her nose out of other people's business.

Chapter Fourteen

Jeagan ate a light breakfast of coffee and a strawberry waffle in Café Espresso the next morning. When she finished, she returned to the hotel lobby and approached the concierge, a young, black man, about her plans to go to Mudd Island. He made the arrangements.

An hour later—dressed in jeans, her Peabody tee shirt with the ducks walking across the front, and tennis shoes—she rode the hotel shuttle to Front Street and boarded a tram that crossed part of the Mississippi River to Mudd Island. She watched towboats and barges hard at work on the River as she crossed.

* * *

The man boarded the next tram after the one Jeagan took. After he arrived minutes behind her, he moved through the small group of passengers and spotted Jeagan. He remained a safe distance behind her as she entered the museum. Minutes later, he also entered the museum and watched as she wandered through the colorful exhibits of River memorabilia. He stood behind a white wooden railing on the floor below her as she stood in front of a lifelike wax figure of Mark Twain, who told stories of life as a boy on the Mississippi. Soon, the man left the museum, afraid that Jeagan might spot him, and found a table at an outdoor café where he could see the museum entrance.

After an hour of Mark Twain's tall tales and a walk on a replica of an old paddle wheeler riverboat—complete with sounds of waves lapping against the sides of the boat, the captain calling out orders to the crew, and the rolling motion of the River—Jeagan left the museum. She took off her tennis shoes and waded in the replica of the River along the River walk while she noted all the towns and cities along its southward route.

When she reached the Gulf of Mexico at the end of the replica, she stopped at Café New Orleans. She sat at a white bistro table outdoors on the tiled patio. The warm morning sun and the brisk breeze from the River washed over her as she studied the menu and air-dried her feet. After she placed her order for red beans and rice, which she had heard about but never tried, she sat back and watched a real paddle wheeler riverboat. The riverboat, filled with what appeared to be tourists, cruised northward up the River.

Suddenly her skin prickled and she again felt that someone was watching her. When she looked around, she saw that the people seated around her were either involved in their own conversations or gazing at the choppy water. No one appeared interested in her. Once again, she realized that her imagination was most likely in overdrive, and she was anxious about her meeting with Isabel.

Jeagan ate and paid for her lunch and put on her shoes. She walked back to the tram.

*   *   *

The man waited until the doors closed on the car she rode in and then stepped from behind a column. He stood in line for the next tram.

*   *   *

Dressed in her new jungle-print outfit and flats, Jeagan arrived at the Orpheum at four o'clock. A former movie theater, the concierge had told her when she asked for directions, the theater had been restored and decorated in grand style with plush red carpeting, sparkling crystal chandeliers, and polished marble stairways. The theater buzzed with activity: maids cleaned lighting fixtures and polished brass, florists arranged vases and baskets of spring flowers, caterers set up tables and covered them in starched white linen, and cast members strolled in and out of the lobby clad in leotards and soft-soled shoes. Others stood around and consulted pages of notes.

"May I help you?"

Jeagan turned and noticed a middle-aged blonde woman—perfectly coiffed and smartly dressed in a turquoise silk-and-wool pantsuit—beside her.

"Oh, yes. I'm here to meet Isabel Lloyd," Jeagan said.

"Let's see," the woman said. She looked around the theater. "She's here somewhere. Yes, that's her over there in the teal dress."

"Thank you," Jeagan said, then looked at the woman, who was Isabel Lloyd, seated in a wheelchair.

Slowly Jeagan, her hands clammy and shaky, walked toward Isabel. As Jeagan drew nearer, she noticed the kind expression of the slight, elderly woman—her short gray hair, smartly styled and fluffed away from her lined but still pretty face—who sat talking with several other women. Isabel might be in a wheelchair, Jeagan noticed, but she radiated an air of confidence and contentment.

Isabel glanced up as Jeagan approached. She excused herself and turned her electric wheelchair toward Jeagan.

"Miss Lloyd?" Jeagan said, hesitantly.

"Yes. You must be the lady who called yesterday?" Isabel extended her hand.

"Yes, I'm Jeagan Christensen." She shook Isabel's hand. "I've come from Denver to talk with you."

"Well, let's go somewhere that's a little quieter."

Jeagan went around to the back of the wheelchair and took the handles.

"That won't be necessary, dear," Isabel said. "It's electric. Let's go into the lounge."

Jeagan followed Isabel into the lounge, which was furnished with plush, tapestry chairs and sofas.

"Your phone call yesterday was rather disturbing," Isabel said when Jeagan sat on a chair in front of her.

Jeagan's words rushed out. "I tried to see you the day before, but your butler told me that you were ill. Your sister said she would talk to you to see if you felt like having a visitor and then

79

call me at the hotel. When I didn't hear from her, I called you. Then, when you hung up the phone, I—"

Isabel raised her hand. "Slow down, dear. I'm sorry about your phone call. What you said about the summer of 1944 was quite a shock. The phone slipped out of my hand. By the time I picked it up, I only heard a dial tone. I debated about calling you back, but I was pretty shaken." Her clear, gray eyes still showed pain after all the years. "As far as being ill, I've had the flu, but I feel much better now."

"I'm glad to hear that. Ms. Lloyd...," Jeagan began nervously.

"Please, call me Isabel."

"Isabel," Jeagan smiled. "This is very hard for me to say, and I know it will sound crazy to you, but I recently bought a desk at an antique store in Denver. After some research on it, I found out that it came from the Peabody Hotel."

"How odd," Isabel said, showing mild interest.

"Yes, it is. The reason I did the research on the desk was because...because I had flashes of...of things that happened to you in 1944 when you were a guest at the hotel." Jeagan watched for Isabel's reaction.

"That's incredible," Isabel said, somewhat skeptical. "What kind of flashes did you have?"

"The first time I sat at the desk, someone called to you to get ready for dinner. You were at the desk, the desk I now own, writing a letter to a friend. I believe her name was Virginia."

"Virginia!"

"Did you have a friend named Virginia?" Jeagan asked, hesitantly.

"Yes, I did and still do—Virginia White, now Robison—but how did you know?" Isabel appeared confused.

"You mentioned that you were writing a letter to her...in the flashback." Jeagan paused to let the information sink in.

"Writing to her? Well, I'm sure I did write to her that summer. I believe she was visiting her fiancé and his family in Centre, Alabama."

Jeagan continued. "The next time I sat at the desk, the flashback I had concerned you and your father. You were arguing about someone named Alan." As Isabel's face drained of color, Jeagan wished she did not have to hurt her this way.

"Alan McCarter," Isabel whispered to herself.

"I'm sorry to upset you like this," Jeagan said. She touched Isabel's hand. "This is something I feel you have to know. It has haunted me and no one else believes me. You are the only person left that it really concerns."

"What else do you have to tell me?" Isabel said. She gripped the handles of the wheelchair and appeared to steel herself for what was to come.

"Well..." Jeagan hesitated. If only she had returned the desk to the antique shop. She had not realized how much hurt she would cause this woman who had suffered so much already.

"Please, go on," Isabel said. "I can see this isn't easy for you, dear, but it must be important for you to come all this way just to find me."

Jeagan took a deep breath, in an attempt to steady herself. She took Isabel's hand between her own. "Isabel, the next flashback I had was of you and Alan at the gazebo."

"In Court Square," Isabel whispered, remembering.

"Yes. He asked you to marry him."

Tears formed in Isabel's eyes.

Jeagan squeezed Isabel's hand. Her heart ached for this woman. "Isabel, after you left the gazebo, your father arrived and threatened Alan."

"My father!"

"Yes, your father. He told Alan to stay away from you. Alan refused and insisted that he would marry you and make you happy."

A smile curved the edges of Isabel's mouth, despite the tears.

Jeagan shifted in her seat. "Then...Oh, God, I hate doing this!"

"Please, tell me what it is," Isabel said.

"Your father shot Alan!" Jeagan blurted out.

"Oh, dear Lord!" Isabel gripped Jeagan's hand and closed her eyes. She sat very still as if holding her breath. Moments later, tears slipped down her cheeks.

"I'm so sorry," Jeagan said softly.

After a while, Isabel released Jeagan's hand and pulled a handkerchief from her handbag. She dried her eyes. "I knew Father hated Alan because he was from a poor family," she said. "He said Alan was not good enough for 'his' daughter—but murder! I can't believe he would kill Alan."

Jeagan's heart broke for this woman. "Isabel, I'm so sorry about coming here to tell you this terrible news. Maybe I should have kept it to myself instead of hurting you like this."

"No, Jeagan, you did what was right," Isabel said. She took a moment to regain her composure. "You've answered some of the questions that have haunted me for all these years. I could never believe that Alan simply disappeared. I knew he was dead." She paused, lost in her thoughts. "We loved each other so much." She looked at Jeagan, with the years of hurt visible in her eyes. "We planned to be married as soon as the war was over. Alan would finish law school, and we would have had a good life together—the three of us."

"Three?"

"Yes. I didn't know it at the time he asked me to marry him, but I was pregnant with his child."

Chapter Fifteen

"My father was furious when he found out that I was pregnant," Isabel said. "He packed me off to a sanitarium in Dovington. He told his friends that I was away studying music in Switzerland." Isabel's voice took on a hard edge. "He couldn't bear the humiliation. Then, when my baby was stillborn, he brought me home and made me promise never to tell anyone that I had been pregnant."

"I had no idea," Jeagan said, shocked. "I can't imagine what you must have gone through, and I'm really sorry to come blasting in here and bring it all up to hurt you again after all these years."

"No, you did what you had to do. At least now I know what really happened to Alan."

"You never married, did you?" Jeagan asked.

"No. I could never have loved anyone the way I loved Alan. I've spent my life doing volunteer work and teaching music. When my father died, he left me the house on Parkway and the summer house in Oxford plus a considerable amount of money. In his later years, he doted on me. After what you've told me, I believe he tried to make amends for what he had done to Alan and me. That's probably why he left me the largest part of his estate."

"Does your sister live with you?" Jeagan asked.

"Yes. After her husband died about three years ago, she came back to live here. She's not close to her children and didn't like living alone. The arrangement was fine with me. That big, old house gets awfully quiet, and it's nice to have Agnes there, although sometimes we clash when she tries to run my life. But, she was wonderful when I had the wreck."

"What happened?" Jeagan asked.

"I'm not really sure. It happened two years ago this May. I was driving down Riverside Drive one evening on my way to visit a friend when a car came from the opposite direction, crossed the center line and came right at me. I panicked and lost control of my car. It rolled over and slid down the embarkment. Fortunately, it stopped before it reached the river or I would have probably drowned. Both my legs were broken as well as my collarbone. That was before I used seat belts, but, as you can probably guess, I'm a firm believer in them now. Anyway, the doctor told me I would never be able to walk again."

"I'm really sorry, Isabel."

"No, need, dear." Isabel smiled. "I've adjusted. I have a van that has been fitted so I can still drive."

Jeagan smiled. "That's wonderful. You're quite a lady."

Isabel sighed. "You do what you have to do in this life, and the good Lord gives you the strength you need when you ask for it." Isabel checked her watch.

"I'm sorry. I'm keeping you, aren't I?" Jeagan said.

"No, you're fine," Isabel said. "I'm the church pianist and have a rehearsal in half an hour."

"Can I help you out to your car?" Jeagan said.

"You can walk with me if you like."

As Jeagan accompanied Isabel out through the back of the theater to the parking lot, she asked. "Was your child a boy or a girl?"

"A boy. I would have named him Alan after...He would have been forty-nine this year in April."

When Isabel was settled into her van, Jeagan said, "Thank you for seeing me, Isabel. I'm sorry to have brought you more hurt, but I just felt that..."

"That's all right, dear." Isabel patted Jeagan's hand that rested on the car door. "Thank you for caring enough to come here. Like I said, at least now I know what really happened to Alan." Isabel paused for a moment. "Look, how would you like to come to the reception and the first performance of *The Phantom of Opera* tonight? I have an extra ticket if you would care to come as my guest."

Jeagan's face brightened. "I'd love to. I missed the performances when *Phantom* was in Denver."

"Wonderful." Isabel turned around in her seat and reached into her handbag. "Here's your ticket. Why don't we meet here around seven? The performance starts at eight."

"Thank you, Isabel. I look forward to it."

Jeagan walked the few blocks back to the hotel with a sense of relief. She had accomplished her mission and could go home. Plus, she had met a very fine lady in the bargain.

She passed a statue of Elvis Presley in front of the Light, Gas, and Water building and smiled. Her hairdresser, Betsy O'Brien, would be green with envy. Betsy was a real fan of The King.

* * *

At seven o'clock, Jeagan entered the Orpheum and handed her invitation to the usher. She wore a low-cut, black crepe dress that she had found in a boutique in the hotel lobby and felt festive with a new French twist hairdo. She accepted a glass of champagne offered by a tuxedoed waiter and then scanned the elegantly dressed and polished crowd that laughed and chatted in the grand lobby.

Isabel was not among the crowd. Jeagan looked for her in the lounge, but she was not there either. Jeagan's watch showed it was only seven-ten—still early. She found an hors d'oeuvre tray and sampled several unidentifiable items to put food into her empty stomach and to pass the time.

"Well, hello."

Jeagan turned to see Edward Coffey standing beside her.

Oh, no, she groaned inwardly. Aloud, she smiled and said, "Hello, Edward."

Edward, dressed in a slightly rumpled dark gray suit and pale gray shirt, grinned and finished off his champagne. He grabbed another glass from the tray of a passing waiter. "So, we meet again."

"Yes, I guess we do," Jeagan said. "Are you here with friends?"

"No," Edward said. He took an hors d'oeuvre from a tray on a table beside him and popped it into his mouth. He looked Jeagan up and down. "You look good enough to..."

Jeagan looked at her watch. "Oh, excuse me, Edward. I've got to find someone before the performance starts. I'll see you later." She walked away.

"But...," Edward said.

Jeagan turned around and waved to him. She moved between groups engaged in theater small talk and situated herself to where she could see the front entrance.

At seven-fifty, the house lights flickered. Isabel still had not arrived. Jeagan began to worry. She followed the crowd as they moved toward their seats in the auditorium. When she found hers, she seated herself but turned around several times to scan the crowd for Isabel. Minutes later the lights went out and the orchestra tuned up to play the overture. Jeagan stood and walked back to the lobby, which was virtually empty by this time. She spotted a phone in the lounge, found Isabel's number in the directory, and called her home.

"Lloyd residence," a female voice answered.

"Yes. This is Jeagan Christensen. Can you tell me if Miss Lloyd has left for the Orpheum? We were to meet here at seven but I haven't seen her."

"Miz Lloyd is out of town, Miz Christensen."

"Out of town?" Jeagan could not believe what she was hearing. "Are you sure? I saw her not four hours ago here at the Orpheum, and she invited me to join her here tonight."

"I'm sorry, Miz Christensen, but she left town an hour ago. A friend of hers is ill, and she took an early evening flight to visit her."

"Oh, I'm sorry to hear that," Jeagan said, disappointed. "Do you expect her to be gone long?"

"I really couldn't say, ma'am. I didn't see her before she left. I was off this afternoon. Miz Harraway told me that she had gone to Alabama to visit Miz Virginia."

"Thank you for your help," Jeagan said and then replaced the receiver. Would Isabel leave town without a call? Although Jeagan had only met her this afternoon, Isabel did not seem the sort of person that would do that. Maybe she had left a message at the hotel. Jeagan dialed.

"Good evening. Peabody Hotel. How may I direct your call?"

"Yes. This is Jeagan Christensen. I'm in room 1004. Do you have any messages for me?"

"One moment, Miss Christensen, and I'll check for you." The operator came back on the line momentarily. "There are no messages for you, ma'am."

"Thank you," Jeagan said.

Frustrated, Jeagan reentered the lobby. The enticing music drew her back to the auditorium. She wanted to see the opera. If Isabel chose to go out of town at the last minute without leaving a message for Jeagan, then so be it. Isabel owed Jeagan nothing. So, she should be able to spend the rest of her time in Memphis enjoying herself and then go home on Saturday. But, what if the uneasiness she felt meant something had happened to Isabel? The only way Jeagan could find out for sure and put her mind at ease would be to try to find Isabel. If she was really in Alabama with a sick friend, then Jeagan could go back inside, watch the opera, and get a decent night's sleep.

Alabama. Isabel had mentioned Alabama when they had talked in the afternoon. Her friend Virginia had visited her fiancé in Centre, Alabama during the summer of 1944. It was a long shot, but the only one Jeagan could think of at the moment. What had Isabel said her friend's name was? Robertson...Robinson...Robison. That was it. Jeagan dialed information for Centre, Alabama and asked for any Robisons. She was given numbers for four Robisons. On her third try, she found Virginia.

"Virginia Robison, please," Jeagan said, when a woman answered the phone.

"This is she," an out-of-breath voice answered.

"My name is Jeagan Christensen. I'm calling from Memphis and I'm trying to find Isabel Lloyd. I was told she was on her way to visit you. Is she there by any chance?"

"Why, no, she isn't here," Virginia Robison said. "Who did you say you were?"

"I'm Jeagan Christensen, a friend of Isabel's." Jeagan explained what had happened.

"I'm sorry, Miss Christensen," Virginia said, "but I haven't seen Isabel in several years, and I'm quite healthy, I assure you. In fact, I was just walking on my treadmill. Anyway, I haven't even talked to Isabel since her birthday last October. Are you sure she's on her way to visit me?"

"That's what I was told, at least that's what I think I was told." Doubts crept into Jeagan's mind.

"Well, why don't you try to call her again. I'm sure there's a good explanation for why she missed the reception. She's a very dependable person."

"Yes, well thank you for your help, Mrs. Robison. Sorry to have bothered you."

"Not at all. Give Isabel my love when you speak to her. Good night."

Jeagan stood for a minute trying to decide what to do. She did not want to pry into Isabel's life any further, but she was afraid something was terribly wrong. Who could help her? Madison. Afterall, he's an attorney, she thought. She searched for his number and dialed.

"Hello?" a male voice said.

"Madison, this is Jeagan Christensen. We met in the Café Espresso?"

"Sure." Jeagan could hear the smile in his voice. "Hi, Jeagan."

"Listen, I'm sorry to bother you," Jeagan said, "but, you're the only person I know in town."

"What's wrong, Jeagan?" Concern edged Madison's voice. "Are you in some kind of trouble?"

"No. It's not me," Jeagan said. "It's a friend of mine. I was supposed to meet her at the Orpheum tonight, and she never arrived. I'm afraid something has happened to her."

"Now, just calm down," Madison said. "Have you tried to call her at home?"

Jeagan told Madison what had happened. "I don't know what to do next. Do you think I should call the police?"

Madison said nothing.

"Madison, are you still there?" Jeagan said.

"Yes," Madison said, his voice cool. He hesitated. "Why don't you come over here so we can discuss this before you call the police? I'm sure your friend's all right and there's a logical explanation."

"Thanks, Madison." Jeagan sighed. "I feel better already. If you'll give me directions, I'll leave now."

"I'm only a few blocks from the Orpheum. Go west on Union and turn south on Front. I'm at the corner of High Pointe and Front." Madison gave her the street address.

Jeagan jotted down the address and hurried out to her car.

The condo was in a gated, riverside community. Jeagan checked in with the guard at the gate and drove through the well-lighted, elegant, beach-style community. Each condo, in various shades of white, cream, peach, gray, or beige stucco, was architecturally unique with wrought-iron courtyards and balconies. Leaves on live oaks rustled in the breeze from the River. Azaleas and dogwoods bordered the condos and bougainvillea vines spilled from many balconies.

Jeagan found Madison's gray stucco condo with bright white trim. Ivy crept up one side of the two-story façade and neatly trimmed shrubs bordered the front walk. At Jeagan's knock, Madison opened the door—dressed in faded jeans, a black knit golf shirt, and white socks.

"Wow! You're a knockout!" he said when he saw her. "I'm sorry you're upset about your friend, but I'm glad you're here." He smiled and put an arm around her shoulder. "Come on in and have a seat. Would you like a drink? Maybe a glass of wine?"

89

Jeagan smiled. "Thanks, Madison, for being here for me. I don't have anywhere else to turn, and yes, I'd love a glass of wine."

"White or red?" he asked.

"I don't care. You choose," Jeagan said.

"Okay. Just have a seat and I'll be right back." He walked noiselessly across the natural oak floor and through the white-carpeted dining room past a black marble table with wrought-iron legs and black-lacquered chairs. A two-tiered, wrought-iron chandelier hung over the table.

Jeagan glanced around Madison's living room, noticing the contemporary black leather couches and glass-top and wrought-iron tables set on a black and white patterned area carpet. She walked over to the wall of windows that faced the River. White drapes tied back with black ties against white walls framed the two-story windows.

"Do you like the view?" Madison asked as he entered the room with two crystal flutes filled with blood-red wine.

"It's fabulous." Jeagan turned to face Madison. "The River looks silver with the moon shining on it. Thank you," she said as she took the offered glass.

"I was really lucky to get this place," Madison said. "I was on a waiting list for two years." He moved to the sofa. "Now, come over here and sit down and tell me what's going on."

Jeagan joined Madison on the couch. She pushed straggling golden strands of hair away from her face. "I guess I'd better start at the beginning. It's going to sound crazy to you, and you might not believe me. Heaven knows, my dad and fiancé don't."

"Fiancé?" Surprise was evident on Madison's face.

"Well, former fiancé is more accurate," Jeagan said. "Anyway, I bought an antique desk in Denver for my new condominium. But, the first time I sat down at it, strange things happened."

"What kind of things?" Madison sipped his wine and settled back on the couch to listen.

"Well...I saw flashes of things that happened to Isabel in 1944."

Madison choked on his wine, nearly spilling his glass. He quickly set his glass on the coffee table.

"Are you all right?" Jeagan said. She reached over and patted his back.

"I'm fine. The wine went down the wrong way. Now, what's this about flashes from the past?"

Jeagan sat back and folded her arms. "I can tell by your eyes that you don't believe me."

"No," Madison said, his brow furrowed in concentration. "No, I'm trying to understand what you're talking about."

"I'm talking about murder." Jeagan stood and crossed the room to the black marble fireplace.

"What do you mean murder? Do you think your friend Isabel murdered someone?"

"Not her, her father murdered someone—Isabel's fiancé. I saw the whole thing."

"When did that happen?" Madison asked.

Jeagan turned to face Madison. "July 13, 1944."

Madison choked again. His eyes narrowed. "Did I hear you right? Did you say 1944?"

"I'm afraid so," Jeagan said, disappointed. "I knew you wouldn't believe me."

"I'm trying to, honestly. That's just too incredible, Jeagan. Did you tell your friend what you saw?"

"Yes, I did," she said. "I've checked everything out and it all fits. She believes me. It was hard for me to tell her what happened since I knew it would hurt her more than she's already been hurt, but I felt she had a right to know."

"You mean to tell me that what you saw in your flashback, or whatever, actually happened?"

"Yes, I think so. She can verify everything except the actual murder."

"But, do you know for sure that her fiancé was actually murdered?" Madison asked.

91

"Well…No, not for sure," Jeagan hesitated. "But Alan was AWOL from his unit after that, and I found an article in the newspaper a month later from his family pleading for information about the their son."

"This is unbelievable," Madison said, shaking his head. "Have you always had this ability to see into the past?"

"No. It's never happened to me before, and I hope it never happens again." Jeagan moved over to sit on the couch again. "Anyway, that's not the point. The point is that I only met Isabel this afternoon. I told her what I had seen and got it all off my chest. It's terrible to say, but I felt relieved that my duty was over. I hoped I could enjoy the rest of my trip and go home with a clear conscience. Now, she's not where she should be, and I feel like it's my fault. What if she's done something crazy? I can only imagine how she felt when I told her about her fiancé's murder. You don't think she'd do anything to hurt herself, do you?"

"No." Madison squeezed Jeagan's hand. "That was a long time ago. I don't think she'd do anything that stupid after all this time. I'm sure nothing has happened to her, and she'll call you tomorrow to apologize for standing you up."

"I certainly hope so." Jeagan looked doubtful. "You think I'm overreacting, don't you?"

Madison scratched his head and looked sheepish. "To be truthful…yes. I do."

"You know, I wonder." Jeagan leaned forward and set her glass on the coffee table. "Isabel said she was involved in a car accident about two years ago. It happened shortly after her sister moved in with her. Maybe I have a suspicious mind, but I wonder if it was really an accident. She said someone crossed the median and forced her off the road. She was nearly killed."

"Now, you really aren't making sense," Madison said. "If someone had tried to kill her, wouldn't they have tried again?"

Jeagan put her head in her hands. "I guess so. I'm mentally and physically exhausted, and then there's this man who's been following me."

"What man?" Madison asked, now alarmed.

"I don't know. He's tall and has sandy-blond hair. I've seen him several times since I arrived in Memphis. I think he's following me."

"Well, I can't say that I blame him." Madison frowned. "Has he approached you in any way?"

"Not really. I keep running into him, literally—yesterday in the park."

"What did he do?" Madison said.

"He grabbed my arm after I ran into him."

"Did you report him to the police or security at the hotel?"

"Well, no." Jeagan raised her head and looked at Madison. "I'm not really sure he is actually following me. Maybe we just happened to be in the same place at the same time—three times yesterday. After I saw him in the park, I drove to Merle, Arkansas to see what I could find out about Alan. I went to see his father…"

"Oh, Jeagan. You didn't?"

"I did. Why shouldn't I?" Jeagan said defensively. "Although I almost regretted going there when I saw Mr. McCarter. He's probably in his nineties. He said he thought I was crazy after I told him that I saw Alan shot by Isabel's father."

Madison laughed. "Can you blame him? It does sound crazy."

"I know it sounds crazy. I'd say the same thing if it hadn't happened to me, but I did see Isabel's father shoot Alan." She hesitated for a moment. "Anyway, I think I saw the sandy-haired man in a brown Taurus parked down the road from Mr. McCarter's. Then, when I got back to the hotel, I saw him drive in the parking garage in a brown Taurus."

"That doesn't make much sense, Jeagan. Why would the guy follow you to Arkansas and just sit and watch you? Are you sure it was the same car? Did you get the license plate number?"

"No, I didn't think of it at the time. I was worried about Mr. McCarter and his reaction to what I told him about Alan."

"Look, Jeagan. You seem really upset about all this." Madison stood. "Why don't you spend the night here? Things will look better in the morning, and I'm sure you'll hear from Isabel tomorrow. Then, we can go down to Beale Street for a fun evening, and you can go back to Denver as planned on Saturday. That is, provided you extend me an invitation to come out and do some skiing around Christmas time."

Jeagan looked up at Madison and smiled. "That would be great. Consider yourself invited. I have a guest room with a great view of the Rockies." Jeagan stood and picked up her handbag from the coffee table. "Thanks for the invitation, but I don't think I'd better stay tonight. If Isabel should try to call me, I'd like to be there."

Jeagan headed toward the door, then paused. "There is one thing you can do for me though. Could you possibly check on that accident Isabel was in? Maybe see if there was anything questionable about it? I know it sounds silly, but I'd feel a lot better if I knew for sure it was really an accident."

"Sure," Madison agreed and followed Jeagan to the door. "I'll be glad to check it out if it'll make you feel any better. I've got a friend at the Memphis Police Department—Sergeant Jim Hylton. I'll call him first thing in the morning."

"Thanks, Madison. I really appreciate your help." Jeagan sighed. "I feel a lot better. Maybe now I'll be able to sleep tonight."

"Glad to help. Sure I can't talk you into staying? I've got a great guest room with a spectacular view of the River."

Jeagan smiled and nodded. "I'm sure."

"Okay. Let me get my shoes, and I'll walk you out to your car. I want to make sure you're locked in tight." He ran up white-carpeted stairs with white balusters and polished oak handrails. Minutes later, he returned wearing tennis shoes.

"You're a real friend," Jeagan said, as they walked outside and over to her car.

"Now." Madison opened the car door for Jeagan. "Keep your doors locked until you get to the hotel. Turn your car over to the valet. Don't park it yourself."

"But, I usually park the car myself," Jeagan protested.

"Not tonight, you don't," Madison said, his face serious.

"Okay, okay." Jeagan laughed. She leaned over and kissed Madison on the cheek before she stepped into her car.

Madison closed and locked the door. "Be careful and get a good night's sleep. I'll give you a call tomorrow."

"Thanks, Madison."

Jeagan started the car, pulled out of her parking space, and turned toward the exit. She waved at Madison, who stood watching her with his hands stuffed in his pockets. She felt calmer, but she still had an uneasy feeling about Isabel.

"I'll never be able to get to sleep tonight, if I don't know she's all right," she said aloud as she turned left onto Front Street.

Jeagan turned right onto Union Avenue, continued past the Peabody, and drove east toward Parkway. She told herself that she would only go by Isabel's and take a look. When Jeagan reached the house, she drove past slowly. Lights were on in several rooms in the main and upper levels. Everything appeared peaceful. Nevertheless, she parked her car on the street several houses away and followed the sidewalk to Isabel's house.

Once on the grounds, she crept around to where the living room was located. Lights were on inside. She edged along the stucco wall and peered in a window.

Agnes stood with her back to the window, the phone in her hand.

Jeagan could hear Agnes speaking loudly, but could only pick out a few words.

"...because she was so upset...need to sedate her...may have to do it soon...her to the country house in Oxford..."

Suddenly, Agnes turned around. Jeagan jumped, afraid she would be seen outside the window. She fell backwards over a hedge and knocked over a pail of water that was left in the yard.

When she scrambled to her feet, she ran toward the street, hoping no one inside the house had heard the crash. It sounded like an explosion to her, and she expected someone to yell at her before she reached her car. As she rounded a flowering crabapple tree, she ran into someone.

Jeagan screamed as an arm grabbed her and a hand went over her mouth.

Chapter Sixteen

"Quiet!" the man said in her ear. "Why are you snooping around here?"

Jeagan struggled to free herself.

"I'll let you go if you'll keep quiet."

Jeagan vigorously nodded her head.

The man let her go.

Jeagan whirled around to see who her attacker was. "You, again!" she said, too angry to be frightened. "Why are you following me?"

"Following you? What are you doing here?" the sandy-haired man said. "Don't you know this is private property? At the rate you're going, you'll find yourself in serious trouble before long."

"Why are you so interested in me?" Jeagan demanded.

"Who said I was interested in you?" the man shrugged. "If you'll tell me what you're up to, I'll try to help you."

"Likely story." Jeagan stomped the man's instep with her heel. He yelped and grabbed his foot.

When she reached her car, she fumbled with her keys and then dropped them. Hands shaking, she moaned and stooped to retrieve them. A quick glance back toward Isabel's house told her the man was running after her. She screamed, jammed the key in the lock, opened the door, and jumped inside. As she reached over and hit the automatic door locks, the man reached the car and grabbed the door handle.

"Open the door. I need to talk to you," the man said.

"Get away from me!" Jeagan screamed. Barely able to hold the keys in her shaking hands, Jeagan managed to insert the key in the ignition, start the car, and shoot away from the curb.

The man jumped out of the way before the back tire caught his foot. He raced back toward the house.

Her whole body shook and tears streamed down her face as Jeagan tore along Parkway and turned right on Union Avenue toward the hotel. After several blocks, she spotted a police station on her right. Tires squealed as she jerked the wheel to the right from the left lane amid honking horns from three cars in the right lanes.

Oblivious to the cars' horns and drivers' curses, Jeagan threw open her car door and ran into the police station. Her breath came in short gasps as she approached a female officer at the front desk.

"I'd like to...report...a kidnapping and a mugging."

The officer's eyes surveyed Jeagan, whose hair straggled down her neck from its French twist and was dotted with leaves from the hedge she had fallen into. Her hands, shoes, and dress were wet and streaked with mud, and her nylons were torn.

"Have a seat, Miss...?"

"Christensen, Jeagan Christensen." She fell into the offered orange plastic chair while she tried to catch her breath.

"Wait right here, Miss Christensen. I'll be right back."

Jeagan nodded and put her head in her hands.

A few moments later, a male officer approached Jeagan. "Miss Christensen?"

Jeagan raised her head to see a man—average height but muscular with salt-and-pepper hair and serious brown eyes.

"I'm Lieutenant Joe Freshour," he said. Jeagan saw the frown wrinkle his brow as he took in her disheveled appearance. "What happened? Were you attacked?"

"Not exactly. He grabbed me, but I stomped on his instep." She shook her head and stood. "But, that's not the important part. They've drugged Isabel and kidnapped her."

"All right. If you'll come with me, I'll see if I can help you." He led Jeagan to his office. "Now, have a seat and tell me what happened. Would you like some coffee?"

"Please," Jeagan said, as she sat in the gray vinyl-and-metal chair in front of Lieutenant Freshour's desk.

The lieutenant left his office and returned minutes later with two cups filled with steaming coffee. He handed one to Jeagan and slowly moved around to the other side of his gray metal desk. He seated himself, drank from his cup, and eyed the young woman seated in front of him.

Jeagan thanked the lieutenant, sipped her coffee—grimaced at the bitterness of it—and set the cup on the edge of the lieutenant's desk.

"Now, tell me what happened," he said. He folded his arms and leaned back in his chair.

"Well, it's a long story."

"Let's hear it."

Jeagan briefly outlined what had taken place since her arrival in Memphis.

The lieutenant interrupted her when she reached the point where Isabel was supposed to have flown to Alabama. "Who told you that Ms. Lloyd had gone to Alabama?"

"Why, the maid who answered the phone when I called Isabel's house. She's the one who told me."

Lieutenant Freshour nodded.

"After I talked to a friend, who assured me I was overreacting, I went out to Isabel's house and looked in a window where I saw her sister, Agnes, talking on the phone. She told the person on the other end of the line that Isabel was upset, obviously by what I told her this afternoon. Then, Agnes said something about sedating Isabel and taking her to the country house in Oxford. I assume she meant Oxford, Mississippi."

"What did you tell Isabel this afternoon?" Lieutenant Freshour asked.

"Well." Jeagan shifted in her chair. She had not wanted to get into this part of what had happened. "I told her that her father killed her fiancé over fifty years ago."

The lieutenant's eyes widened. "How do you know that?"

"I don't have time to explain all that right now," Jeagan said. "You'll have to trust me. Anyway, that's not the point and besides her father is dead. The point is that I believe Isabel has been kidnapped and we've got to find her!" Jeagan's hand shook as she reached for the coffee cup.

"Just calm down, Miss Christensen."

"Jeagan."

"All right, Jeagan," the lieutenant said. "I'll check on her myself. Do you have her home number?"

"No, but the listing is Isabel Lloyd on Parkway." Jeagan sat straighter in her chair. Maybe someone actually believed her and would help.

Lietutenant Freshour located the number in the Memphis directory and dialed.

"Lloyd residence," a voice answered on the other end of the line.

"This is Lieutenant Joe Freshour of the Memphis Police Department. May I speak with Isabel Lloyd?"

"Uh...I'm sorry, Lieutenant. Miz Lloyd's not at home."

"To whom am I speaking?"

"I'm Ellie Bracken, sir, Miz Isabel's maid."

"Ms. Bracken, where can I reach Miss Lloyd?"

"Well, sir, Miz Harraway told me that Miz Isabel went to visit a sick friend, but I musta misunderstood because I heard her tell somebody on the phone a little while ago that she's gone down to the country house in Oxford."

"I see," Lieutenant Freshour said. "Is Mrs. Harraway available to speak with me?"

"I'll check and see if you'll hold on for jes a minute," Ellie said.

"Thank you." Lieutenant Freshour covered the mouthpiece. "The maid has gone to find Mrs. Harraway. Who is she?"

"She's Isabel's sister, Agnes Harraway," Jeagan said.

"Hello?" The lieutenant noted that the new voice on the other end of the line sounded hesitant.

"Yes. Mrs. Harraway, this is Lieutenant Joe Freshour, Memphis Police Department. I have a Miss Christensen here in my office."

Jeagan gasped. "No! Don't tell her that!"

The lieutenant motioned for Jeagan to be quiet.

"I see," Agnes Harraway said coolly.

"Uh. Mrs. Harraway, can you tell me where I can reach your sister?" the lieutenant said.

"Of course, I can, Lieutenant. She's at our country house in Oxford. The butler took her there earlier this evening. Is there a problem?"

"Well, it seems she had an appointment to meet Miss Christensen at the Orpheum Theater tonight, and when she didn't arrive for the performance, Miss Christensen became worried."

"Yes. I believe the maid told me that Miss Christensen called earlier. Isabel was truly sorry to have to miss the reception and performance, but she is still recovering from a bout of flu and decided to go down to the country house for a few days of fresh air and sunshine. She said to give Miss Christensen her regrets if she called."

"Thank you, Mrs. Harraway. Just one other thing," the lieutenant said. "Miss Christensen said she was told earlier that Miss Lloyd had left town to visit a sick friend."

"Yes," Agnes said. "The maid misunderstood what I told her. I apologize for the mix-up, Lieutenant. If Miss Christensen needs to talk with my sister, she can reach her in Oxford in the morning."

"Thank you for your help, ma'am. I'm sure Miss Christensen will understand. Good night."

Lieutenant Freshour replaced the receiver. Jeagan noticed the creases between his eyebrows deepen, but his expression told Jeagan nothing.

"Well?" Jeagan asked, sitting on the edge of her chair.

"Mrs. Harraway says her sister is at the country house in Oxford and that you can reach her there tomorrow," Lieutenant Freshour said slowly, as if to a child. "She also said her sister was sorry to have missed the performance tonight, but needed to get away for a few days of fresh air and sunshine. Mrs. Harraway also apologized for the mix-up about Miss Lloyd's whereabouts."

"I'll bet she did," Jeagan said, her eyes bright. "I think she's lying. I think Isabel has been taken somewhere against her will.

While I was listening at the window, I believe I heard her say something about having to do something soon."

Lieutenant Freshour stood. "Now, Miss Christensen—Jeagan—don't start jumping to conclusions. Get some rest tonight. I'll call her tomorrow if it will make you feel any better, and I'll let you know what I find out. Now, what's this about a man attacking you?"

"I...," Jeagan slumped back in her seat. "He didn't exactly attack me. He told me that I was going to get myself into trouble."

"Where were you when he said this?" the lieutenant asked.

"I...," Jeagan said sheepishly, "I was in Isabel's front yard."

Lieutenant Freshour placed his hands on his desk. "It appears this man told you what you should have already known. You were trespassing. The Lloyds could press charges against you."

"But, what was he doing there?" Jeagan asked. "I don't think he lives there. He was following me."

"Maybe he works for the Lloyds. Did you ask him that?"

"Well...no. I didn't ask him that." Jeagan couldn't think. Maybe the sandy-haired man did work for the Lloyds, and she only ran into him in the park by chance. She straightened in her chair. "If he works for the Lloyds, why did I run into him three times yesterday?"

The lieutenant's eyebrows rose. "Three times?"

Jeagan nodded. "I literally ran into him in Court Square park yesterday, and then I think I saw him again in Merle, Arkansas, and again in the parking garage at the Peabody Hotel. I think he's stalking me."

"You think you saw him in Merle, Arkansas. You're not sure?"

"Well, not exactly sure," Jeagan looked down at her hands. She tried to pick some of the dried mud off her fingers. "But I really think it was him."

The lieutenant sighed. "All right, give me a description of the man. We'll alert the security guard at the hotel."

Jeagan looked up, a hopeful expression on her face. "He's over six feet, sandy-blond hair, broad shoulders. Uh...I believe he was wearing khakis and a light blue shirt...maybe a golf shirt."

After writing down the description, the lieutenant stood. "I'll be right back."

Jeagan closed her eyes and took slow, deep breaths.

Minutes later the lieutenant returned. "I'll have an officer drive you to the Peabody," he said.

"My car is outside. It's a rental and I don't want to leave it here. Anyway, I'm okay to drive."

The lieutenant was insistent. "We'll have someone drive your car back to the hotel. I don't believe you're in any condition to drive. Just try to get some rest tonight."

Jeagan was too exhausted to argue, even if the lieutenant did sound like her dad or Brandon. She pulled herself up from the chair and walked through the station and outside with Lieutenant Freshour.

"Sergeant Fields, please drive this lady to the Peabody," the lieutenant said. "Have Officer Crowe follow you in her car. Also, give this description to Ken Rockwell in Hotel Security. This man may be stalking Miss Christensen."

Sergeant Fields——twenty-fivish, short, and solid—nodded and opened the patrol car door for Jeagan.

Jeagan turned to the lieutenant. Maybe he did believe her after all. "Thank you," she said, and extended her hand. "You'll call me in the morning after you talk to Isabel?"

"Absolutely." Lieutenant Freshour closed the car door and smiled at Jeagan. "Good night."

Chapter Seventeen

A police escort into the lobby of the Peabody brought Jeagan attention she didn't want. She passed a mirror and saw her reflection—she looked as if she had been in a fight with an alley cat...and lost.

Sergeant Fields approached the front desk—Jeagan stayed behind him in an attempt to hide from the desk clerk—and asked for Ken Rockwell. The desk clerk looked around the policeman and spotted Jeagan. A disapproving grimace spread across the clerk's face as she looked Jeagan over. The clerk paged the Security Officer on his beeper.

At the insistence of the desk clerk, Jeagan and Sergeant Fields waited for Ken Rockwell in an office behind the front desk. Jeagan understood the clerk wanting to hustle her out of the lobby, considering the way she looked.

Ken Rockwell arrived within minutes—a stocky, red-haired man with a bushy mustache and eyebrows to match—dressed in a gray polyester jacket and open-necked white shirt. When he saw Jeagan, he recognized her as a guest. "What happened?" he asked the sergeant.

Before the sergeant could say anything, Jeagan spoke up. She explained the situation, offering only sketchy information, then described the sandy-haired man and provided details of the times she had seen him.

Rockwell took notes in a black notebook. "How long do you plan to be in Memphis?"

"I plan to leave on Saturday, if not before," Jeagan answered. "The way things are going, I want to get out of here as soon as I can. That is, as soon as I know Isabel Lloyd is okay." She pushed her hair out of her eyes and tried unsuccessfully to tuck the trailing locks back into the French twist.

Rockwell's forehead wrinkled in puzzlement. "I'm confused. What does this Isabel Lloyd have to do with the sandy-haired man?"

Jeagan straightened in her chair, once again alert. "I have no idea. I had never seen the man before I visited Isabel's home on Tuesday. But, the very next morning — Wednesday— I ran into him several times in places that I don't think he would have been unless he was following me. I tried to tell myself that seeing him so many times was a coincidence, until I ran into him outside Isabel's tonight."

Rockwell shifted in his chair. "Maybe this guy works for the Lloyds, and when he spotted you on their property…"

Jeagan shook her head. "I've been through all that with the lieutenant. That would seem reasonable except that I saw the man in Court Square and then in Merle, Arkansas yesterday and then in the hotel parking garage. That's too many coincidences."

Sergeant Field spoke up. "You're probably right. That is too many coincidences. I'll check with Lieutenant Freshour when I get back and see if we can question the Lloyds about this man."

"Good idea," Rockwell said. "I'll give the staff here his description." He smiled reassuringly at Jeagan. "If he's on hotel property, we'll find him."

Jeagan felt safe. These two men seemed concerned about her—more so than the other two men in her life that she had left behind in Denver.

Sergeant Fields escorted Jeagan out of the office, while Ken Rockwell made a series of phone calls that would alert the hotel staff.

As she crossed the lobby, Jeagan spotted Edward Coffey. He sat with two other men and was about to take a drink out of the glass in his hand when he stopped. His mouth dropped open. Jeagan glared at him. Edward turned his head, as if he had not seen her.

Jeagan smiled. Good, she thought. He probably thinks I'm in trouble with the police. That should keep him away from me.

After riding the elevator to the tenth floor with Jeagan, Sergeant Fields walked down the hall with her, unlocked her door, and searched the room before he let her step inside. Satisfied that no one was in her room, he let Jeagan enter and made her promise to chain lock the door after he left.

That was not a problem for Jeagan.

"Thanks, Sergeant," she said, as she extended her hand.

"You're welcome. Now, if you hear anything suspicious, just call Rockwell or call me at the precinct, and I'll be here in five minutes." Fields fished in his wallet for a card and handed it to Jeagan.

"I feel much better now. You've been awfully nice about this, Sergeant. I know I probably look and sound like a nut, but..."

He raised his hand as if to ward off her words. "No, you don't sound like a nut, although you do look a little strange for a lady who has just been to the opera." He grinned, his sky-blue eyes twinkling.

Jeagan laughed and pushed her hair out of her eyes. "You're right."

She closed and locked the door behind the policeman, then inserted the chain lock into place. She sighed. Sergeant Fields was awfully nice and cute...and young, she thought. After surveying the room, she went over and pulled out the desk chair, which she placed in front of the door. "For noise," she told herself. "If someone tries to get in, at least I'll hear him."

Jeagan went into the bathroom and peeled off her mud-stained dress and torn nylons. She washed the dirt from her hands and legs, then took her hair down from the French twist and combed it out. Her reflection in the vanity mirror looked tired and drawn. "You look a hundred years old," she told her reflection. "You've got to get out of this town before you get yourself killed."

Chapter Eighteen

The jangling of the phone startled Jeagan awake the next morning at eight o'clock. She propped herself on her elbow and reached for the phone. Half awake, she said, "Hello?"

"Good morning, Miss Christensen. This is Bryan Yust. I hope I didn't wake you." His voice was too loud and too crisp. Jeagan held the phone away from her ear.

"I'm awake," she said still groggy.

"Well, I have some good news for you. I've just talked with our accountant, and he said we can allow you to review our archived records. When you're ready, I'll take you to our storage area in the basement."

Jeagan stuttered. "Uh...well...Thanks for getting back to me, but I won't need to see the records after all."

"Oh," Yust said, surprise and disappointment evident in his voice.

"I'm sorry," Jeagan said. "I should have called you yesterday to let you know."

"Well, that's all right," Yust said. "As long as you're sure, since I've gotten approval for you."

"I'm sure, but thank you anyway for your trouble." The man sounded positively hurt, she thought. Hopefully, gaining her access to the records area would not have been the highlight of his week. She moved to get out of bed and felt the soreness of her hip where she had fallen over the bucket in Isabel's yard. She rubbed the spot and pulled herself out of bed. As she headed toward the bathroom, the phone rang again. She groaned and walked back to the nightstand to answer it.

"Hello?"

"Miss Christensen, this is Lieutenant Freshour."

Jeagan sat on the bed, suddenly awake. "Oh, Lieutenant. Good morning. Have you talked to Isabel?"

"Yes. I talked to her a few minutes ago. She sounded fine and asked me to tell you how sorry she was for not making it to the performance last night. She said the news you gave her was just too much, and she didn't feel well enough to attend the ballet."

"The what?" Jeagan said, startled.

"What did you say?" Lieutenant Freshour asked.

"I asked you what she said she couldn't attend?"

"She said the ballet."

"But, there was no ballet last night," Jeagan said, her skin prickling. "It was an opera."

"Well, maybe she was still asleep when I called or she was a little confused."

"I don't think so," Jeagan said. "Her mind seemed as sharp as yours or mine when I talked to her yesterday. It sounds to me like she was trying to let you know everything was not all right. What else did she say?"

"Well, she said she was sorry for the misunderstanding about visiting her friend in Virginia."

Jeagan's eyes widened. "Lieutenant! Her friend is named Virginia. She doesn't live in Virginia. She lives in Centre, Alabama. I really think Isabel was trying to get a point across to you that something's wrong."

"Now, I don't think we need to jump to any conclusions, Miss Christensen. Like I said, she sounded fine to me. She said she would be staying in Oxford through the weekend, and hoped to be her old self by Monday."

"Lieutenant!" Jeagan said, now really worried. "That's something else. She plays the piano on Sundays at her church. In fact, she had a rehearsal yesterday afternoon."

"Just calm down. Maybe you're right, but I doubt it. Tell you what, I'll call and check on her again around noon and let you know how she sounds then, if that'll make you feel better."

"Thanks. That will make me feel a lot better."

After she hung up the phone, Jeagan showered, braided her hair, dressed in her black-and-white slacks, white shirt, and black flats, and then left the hotel. She crossed Union Avenue and had breakfast at a pancake house, hoping to avoid running into either the sandy-haired man or the pesky Edward Coffey.

She ordered Belgian waffles and glanced over the newspaper while she drank hot coffee, but the caffeine did little to lift her spirits. She tried not to worry about Isabel. After all, Lieutenant Freshour was in charge of the situation now. There was nothing more that she could do. When she looked outside, she noticed for the first time what a beautiful, sunny day it was. Too bad she did not feel like enjoying it.

Jeagan's attention returned to the paper. The headlines showed that a baby had been found in a dumpster behind an apartment complex. Thankfully, the baby was still alive, but severely dehydrated. She shook her head, wondering how anyone could be that evil. Then, a thought occurred to her. What if...?

Jeagan pulled out her billfold and left money on the table for her breakfast. As she got up to leave, the waitress arrived with her order. "I'm sorry. I have to leave," Jeagan said.

The waitress, wearing a too-tight uniform and an attitude, looked after Jeagan. "Whatever," the waitress mumbled disgustedly as she pocketed the money and carried the plate back into the kitchen.

Back in the hotel, Jeagan approached the black concierge. "Good morning," he said, recognizing Jeagan.

"Hello," Jeagan said. "I need your help again. I need a Tennessee map."

The concierge smiled. "Where are you traveling today?"

"Dovington. Can you tell me how far it is?"

"Let's see." He opened a Tennessee map and traced a route for Jeagan.

Jeagan thanked the man and took the elevator back to her room to get her car keys. When she retrieved her keys, she noticed her message light. She dialed the operator.

"This is Jeagan Christensen in room 1004. You have a message for me?"

"Yes," the operator said. "Madison Hannah called and would like for you to call him."

Jeagan scribbled the number on a pad and dialed Madison's number.

"Madison Hannah," he answered in a businesslike tone.

"Hi, Madison. It's Jeagan."

Madison's tone changed immediately. "Hi yourself. I hope you feel better than you did last night."

"Not really," Jeagan said. "The rest of my night was worse than when I saw you."

"What happened? Didn't you go back to the hotel?"

"Well, not exactly. I made a little detour." Jeagan recounted the previous night's events that took place after she left Madison.

When she finished, Madison said, "You took an awful chance trespassing like that." Apparently in an attempt to lighten the conversation, he laughed and added, "Hey, I bargained for dinner tonight, not defending you in court."

"Oh, I forgot all about dinner," Jeagan said.

"Boy, I must have made some impression on you," Madison said. "You've forgotten our date already."

"No. I mean, yes. I did forget, but only for the moment." She laughed. "I'm sorry, Madison. My mind is running in ten different directions. And, yes, I'm looking forward to spending my last evening in Memphis with you."

"Good. I think we'll have fun. I should be through in court around four-thirty. Meet you in the Peabody lobby around five?"

"Sounds great," Jeagan said.

"Oh, before I forget. I contacted my friend Jim Hylton."

Puzzled, Jeagan said, "Jim Hylton?"

"You remember. The Sergeant with the Memphis Police Department?"

"Sorry again," Jeagan said. "I must be losing my mind. What did he tell you about Isabel's accident?"

"He told me that it was just that—an accident. No reason to suspect foul play."

"Well, that's a relief. I sure appreciate you checking for me."

110

"Not a problem," Madison said. 'What are your plans for today? Want to stop by for a tour of my office? The view is terrific. Then, I could take you to lunch at the Petroleum Club on the top of the..."

"No, but thanks, Madison. I'm driving to Dovington to check out something Isabel told me."

"Well, drive carefully. There are some really lousy drivers out there."

Jeagan picked up her keys. Madison was turning out to be a good friend, she thought. When she opened the door, she spotted Edward in the hall. He was closing his door.

"Hi," he said, inserting his key in his pocket. "Are you okay?"

"I'm fine. Thanks," she said and turned toward the elevators.

"Hey," Edward caught up to her. "I didn't mean to ignore you when I saw you with that cop last night, but I..."

"That's okay. It was only a misunderstanding. I don't think I'll have to do any jail time," Jeagan said, trying not to laugh.

Edward's eyebrows rose. "Jail time!"

"Yes. The sergeant told me that the man I stole the wallet from wouldn't press charges if I returned it. He didn't want any publicity—you know, a family and all."

"Oh, I see." Edward pressed the down button when they reached the elevator. He patted his back pocket and seemed relieved when he felt the bulk of his wallet. He said nothing when they entered the elevator. He kept his eyes to the front, and when the elevator reached the lobby, he nodded to Jeagan. "After you."

Jeagan exited the elevator. Edward followed her, then said, "Have a good day." He scampered off toward the front doors of the hotel and was out on the sidewalk before Jeagan could cross the lobby.

She laughed out loud. She would have to remember that line the next time a married man made a pass at her. Edward would probably be no further problem to her.

Jeagan exited the hotel through the rear doors. She noticed that her car was in real need of washing as she approached it in the garage. No time for that. She got in and consulted her map. She failed to see the brown Taurus pull out from its parking place on the street as she left the hotel.

Chapter Nineteen

The drive to Dovington took Jeagan through Frayser where she had met the first Isabel Lloyd. The community was small, but the homes appeared neat and well maintained. Most were surrounded by mature trees, which Jeagan envied. The arid climate of Colorado was not conducive to growing tall, lush, oaks and maples.

As she passed through Millington, Jeagan remembered that the Naval Air Station there was where Alan McCarter should have reported back to his unit. Poor Alan, she thought. What a waste.

Jeagan's thoughts returned to Isabel's baby. The article about the baby in the newspaper made her wonder about baby Alan. Had the baby actually died at birth? He probably had, but a question tickled the back of Jeagan's mind and she had to find out for herself. The vital statistics department in Dovington should have a death certificate or a record of the baby's birth.

When she arrived in Dovington, Jeagan circled the town square and parked in front of the county building. She got out of her car and looked around. The pace of the town seemed slow compared to Denver and Memphis. People appeared content and in no hurry, whether they ambled along the street or sat on park benches under towering oaks. In the town square, she noticed two elderly, gray-haired men, who sat on a bench under the statue of a man on horseback. The horseman appeared to be a Confederate soldier.

Jeagan wished she had her camera with her. The town reminded her of a scene out of a 1950s movie. One man who sat on the bench was dressed in a green-plaid shirt and overalls. He dipped his pipe into a pouch and tamped the tobacco down with his finger. The other man, who wore a red shirt and khaki pants, sat back with his arms folded across his chest, his eyes closed. Jeagan smiled. Would her life ever be that peaceful? Not if she kept nosing into other people's business, it wouldn't.

She climbed the concrete steps to the old county building and entered a long, dark corridor. Her heels clicked on the marble floor as she passed massive doors, stained dark with frosted glass inserts. A directory on the wall near the stairs indicated that the vital statistics office was on the second floor.

The wooden stairway creaked and moaned as she climbed. When she reached the vital statistics office, she approached the counter.

A sixtyish woman, with gray hair pulled into a knot on top of her head, eyed Jeagan as she entered the office. "May I help you?" the woman said. Her expression indicated that helping Jeagan was not what she wanted to do at that particular moment.

"Yes," Jeagan said. She approached a dark, wooden counter with swinging doors at both ends. The office was brightly lit with fluorescent bulbs. "I'd like to find out about a child that was born here in April of 1945. His mother's name was Isabel Lloyd."

In a bored voice, the clerk asked, "What was the child's name?"

"I believe the child was stillborn, but his name would have been Alan if he had lived."

"Then what is it you want to know?" the clerk asked, obviously annoyed.

"I'd like to know if there is a record of his birth?"

"It would take several hours to dig through our records to find that information and…"

"That's fine," Jeagan said. "I'll wait. This is very important information that I need in—in a murder investigation."

The clerk's curiosity now appeared piqued. "Oh, are you a policewoman or a private investigator?"

"No. Well, yes, I guess you could call me a private investigator."

The woman frowned, but took down all the information Jeagan could give her. When the clerk had all the information she required, Jeagan thanked her and left the building in search of a restaurant.

There was nothing she could do now but wait, so she decided to have lunch considering that it would be a long drive back to Memphis. She wandered down the sidewalk, past an insurance company, a laundry, an attorney's office, a real estate office, and a bank. Then, she spotted Edwina's Restaurant.

Edwina, Jeagan soon found out, was a large, cheerful woman with teased auburn hair and a loud voice. She greeted Jeagan as she entered the restaurant. "Good morning, honey. You're a little late for breakfast, but we've got a great blue plate special for lunch."

Jeagan smiled, vaguely reminded of K-Mart's Blue Light Special. "What's the special?"

Edwina guided her across gray linoleum to a booth upholstered in red vinyl. "Today we have chicken and dumplings, with black-eyed peas, fresh tomatoes, and cornbread."

"I've never had dumplings," Jeagan said, "but I'll try them."

Edwina grinned. "You'll love 'em. How 'bout a big glass of just-made iced tea?"

"Okay. Thanks."

"That'll be right out," Edwina said. She dropped off a ticket at the window into the kitchen and headed back toward the door where she greeted two elderly women who had entered the restaurant. So far, everyone in the town appeared friendly except for the clerk in the vital statistics office.

Jeagan opened the napkin with silverware wrapped inside. When a waitress brought her iced tea, she started to add sugar.

"It's already sweetened, honey," the waitress said.

"Oh, thanks," Jeagan said. She sipped her tea and remembered that she had heard somewhere that southerners pre-sweetened their tea. What if she did not like sweet tea, would she have to do without?

Jeagan shook her head. Tea was not the issue here. She had to find out for herself what happened to Isabel's baby. The baby may have been stillborn, but it was also possible that he had lived. If he lived, then Isabel's father had lied to her and most likely given up her son for adoption. Jeagan could well imagine Robert Lloyd doing that to avoid the embarrassment of an illegitimate grandchild.

Isabel said, Jeagan recalled, that in his later life, her father had tried to make amends for ruining her life. Possibly he was trying to assuage his guilt for killing Alan and kidnapping Isabel's baby by leaving the largest part of his estate to Isabel instead of to her sister.

Isabel's sister. Jeagan remembered her statement to someone on the phone about having to do something now. Possibly she was attempting to make Isabel think she was an invalid so she would feel she needed her, or maybe Agnes planned to get rid of Isabel. Jeagan had no way of knowing, but she was worried about Isabel. She considered calling Lieutenant Freshour, but it was not yet noon, and he had said he would call after he talked to Isabel around noon. Maybe Jeagan should allow him to handle the situation and let it go, but she knew she could not.

Minutes later, a plate of steaming chicken and dumplings arrived. "Here you go, dear," Edwina said. She set the plate in front of Jeagan. "Enjoy."

"Thank you. It smells wonderful," Jeagan said. She was glad she had skipped breakfast.

Edwina patted Jeagan on the back. "Let me know if you need a refill on your iced tea."

Jeagan looked at the huge glass and laughed. "Looks like I already have a gallon or so in that glass, so I don't think I'll need any more."

Edwina grinned. "Well, let me know if you need anything else, hon." She headed for the front door again as a tall, fortyish man in a tan suit entered the restaurant. "Hello, counsellor," Edwina said. "Court let out early today?"

"No," he said smiling. "The jury was hungry so they returned an early verdict of guilty so we could get out of the courthouse and get some lunch."

Edwina's booming laughter filled the restaurant. "Good one, counsellor. How about a plate of chicken and dumplings?"

The attorney sat at a window table and looked up at Edwina. "That's what I came in here for."

While she ate, Jeagan watched and listened to the banter between the attorney and Edwina. What an interesting little town, she thought. Friendly people and great food. She ate with gusto and forgot her problems for the moment. She finished her lunch, turned down fresh, hot banana pudding, and then headed back to the courthouse.

Two hours to the minute after Jeagan had left the vital statistics office, she reentered it. The clerk who had helped her previously was not in the office. A black woman, with gray hair and skin the color of smooth milk chocolate, approached the counter.

"May I help you?" she said. Jeagan could tell by her eyes that she meant it.

Jeagan repeated her request. The woman nodded. "Yes. I did the research for Velma." The woman walked over to her desk and retrieved a piece of paper. "Velma had a doctor's appointment and had to leave," she added by way of explanation.

Jeagan nodded and wished the woman would hurry. She seemed to take a long time to retrieve a piece of paper from her desk.

The woman reviewed the document that she held before she returned to the counter. "I'm afraid that what I've found won't be of much help."

Jeagan's face fell. "What did you find?"

The woman shook her head. "We don't have any record of an Isabel Lloyd giving birth here in April of 1945, and there weren't any stillbirths during that month either."

"Well...," Jeagan said, disappointed. "I appreciate your time anyway." She turned to leave.

"I'm sorry I couldn't help you," the woman said. "You can have the list if you want it."

"Sure. Thanks for your time." Jeagan said as she turned back toward the counter. She took the offered document, folded it, and dropped it into her handbag. Discouraged, she wondered if she had been mistaken about Isabel being sent to Dovington. On impulse, she turned back to the counter. The clerk had started back to her desk.

"Excuse me?" Jeagan said.

The clerk stopped and turned around to face Jeagan. "Yes?"

"Is there a sanitarium in Dovington?"

"Yes, ma'am. There's a hospital and sanitarium out on Polk Road."

Jeagan asked for directions and then returned to her car. Maybe Isabel's father had registered her under another name, and maybe someone at the sanitarium might be willing to help her find out if he had.

Highway 57 cut through rolling green hills with white-clapboard farmhouses scattered every few miles on grassy meadows dotted with peacefully grazing brown-and-white cattle. Jeagan breathed deeply of the fresh, spring, country air and tried to relax. Fifteen minutes later she turned off on Polk Road and soon spotted Blake's Hospital and Sanitarium on her left. A white, rambling, two-story clapboard house, it sat in a clearing, surrounded by a variety of towering pines, maples, oaks, and magnolia.

Jeagan entered the long drive bordered by maples that allowed only dappled sunlight through, which flickered on her windshield. The familiar smell of freshly cut grass drifted in the window as she neared the main entrance. As she looked around the grounds, she noticed white, wooden, Adirondack chairs and cushioned benches scattered across the wide front lawn in seating areas beneath the massive trees. If she ever had to be sent to a sanitarium, which might be any day now, this would be the type of place she would choose. It quitely spoke of serenity and peace.

The parking lot was full, but someone pulled out as she entered. She parked her car and followed the red brick path across the lawn to the wide, pale green front porch that stretched around both sides of the building. She noticed white rockers and two swings on the porch that swayed gently in the afternoon breeze.

* * *

He waited until Jeagan was on the front porch before he pulled into the parking lot. He drove slowly to the end of the parking area where she would not be able to spot his car when she came out of the hospital. He rolled down the windows, turned off the ignition, and waited.

* * *

Jeagan opened the screen door and entered the foyer. To her right, stairs with a polished mahogany handrail ran in a smooth curve to the second floor. The dark-stained hardwood foyer lead to an office on the right where Jeagan noticed two desks set against pale blue walls. A young blonde woman dressed in a dark blue business suit and a silky white blouse sat at one of the desks.

"Good morning," the woman said as she rose from her chair. She glanced at her watch and laughed. "Well, I guess it's already afternoon."

"I guess it is," Jeagan said, noting the time. It was nearly one o'clock. She should call Lieutenant Freshour soon. She looked at the young woman. "I need some help."

"Have a seat," the woman said and indicated blue floral chairs in front of her polished pecan desk. "I'm Marcie Graves. I'll see what I can do to help you."

Jeagan felt oddly reassured and at ease. "I'm Jeagan Christensen. I have a strange request. I'd like to find out about a child that was born in Dovington in 1945. I believe the mother may have stayed here during her pregnancy."

"Mmm. That was a long time ago," Marcie said.

"Yes. I know, but I really need to find out about this child. I believe he might have been stillborn."

119

Marcie sat in her desk chair and shook her head. "I'm sorry, but we aren't allowed to give out patient information without a signed release."

"I don't want medical information. I only want to know if the child was born here."

"Well, I don't know." Marcie hesitated, thoughtful. "I could get into a lot of trouble for giving out information without a signed release form."

"How much trouble could there be?" Jeagan held out her hands, palms up. She continued before Marcie could say anything else. "We're talking almost fifty years ago. I'm sure many of your patients from back then have died."

Marcie appeared to weigh Jeagan's request. "How old would the woman have been at the time of the child's birth?"

"About twenty-one. This information is very important, Marcie. It may be a matter of life and death." Well, it could be, Jeagan thought.

Marcie seemed to make a decision. "Okay. I'll see what I can do."

Jeagan smiled and let out her breath. "Thanks, Marcie."

"What was the mother's name?" Marcie reached for a pad and pen.

"Her name was Isabel Lloyd."

"And, you say she gave birth when?"

"April of 1945. She had a son who would have been named Alan."

Marcie scribbled on the paper and then ripped the page from her pad. She moved around to the front of her desk. "Frances Hall in our records area has been here since 1950. If there's a record of Isabel Lloyd being here, she'll find it. I'll be back in a few minutes. Help yourself to some coffee." She indicated a table with a coffee pot and paper cups.

"No, thanks. I just had a huge glass of iced tea with lunch at Edwina's."

Marcie smiled and held up her hand as if to stop traffic. "Say no more. I'm familiar with Edwina's humongous glasses of tea."

120

Jeagan sat for a few minutes after Marcie left the office. Then, hearing noises, Jeagan's curiosity got the better of her. She stood and looked out the door. The sounds of dishes and silverware clanging came from the other end of the hall. The patients must be eating lunch, she thought. She wandered along the hallway and ventured a look into the dining room. Inside, she noticed three rows of square tables, neatly laid with pale blue tablecloths, and matching chairs set against blue and white floral wallpaper above white wainscoting. The interior decorator for this place must have really liked blue, Jeagan thought. The people eating in the dining room, she noticed, ranged in ages from bushy-haired teens to white-haired men and women.

Someone tapped Jeagan on the shoulder. "May I help you?"

Startled, Jeagan jumped and then turned to face a tall, broad black man dressed in white pants and shirt. He appeared none too pleased to see Jeagan peeking into the dining room.

"Oh. I'm sorry," Jeagan said guiltily. "I was waiting for Marcie and I...uh...heard noises and came down the hall to see what was going on."

The man's frown softened slightly. "It would probably be better if you waited in the front office."

"That's fine." Jeagan turned and started back toward the office. She knew the man was following her. She half turned. "This building is lovely."

"The patients like it," he said. He was one step behind her.

When Jeagan was again seated in the front office, the man seemed satisfied and left her there. She watched him walk back down the hall toward the dining area. The patients should feel safe with him around, she thought.

Ten minutes later, Marcie returned with a sheet of paper. "Sorry I took so long."

"That's okay," Jeagan said. "Did you find anything?"

"The only twenty-one-year-old patient who gave birth in April of 1945 was Jane Koehler."

Another dead end. "Did any other women give birth during that month?"

Marcie referred to her list. "Only two others. Both women were in their late twenties, and neither of them was named Lloyd."

"May I have the list?" Jeagan said.

Marcie hesitated. "I…uh…okay." She handed the list to Jeagan.

"Thanks, Marcie. I appreciate your help."

"Sorry I couldn't do more," Marcie said.

Jeagan returned to her car. After she got in and stowed her handbag on the passenger seat, she ran her finger down the list of births in April of 1945. Her finger stopped. She ran her finger across the page. It read: "Jane Koehler. Age: 21. Residence: Memphis, Tennessee. Gave birth at: 6: 20 a.m. Infant: Alan Koehler. Alan! Weight: 7 pounds, 15 ounces. Length: 21 inches. Other: live birth. "Live birth!" Somehow this had to be the key to the whole thing. I was right, Jeagan thought. It was too convenient that Isabel's baby was stillborn.

Robert Lloyd had obviously admitted Isabel under a false name, but the baby at least got to keep his father's name, as Isabel would have wished. That is, before baby Alan was taken away from her. What had her father done with the baby? The record said the baby was alive.

Jeagan stuffed the list into her handbag and drove back to town. She stopped at a gas station, where she filled the car's tank, and then pulled out her cell phone. She retrieved Lieutenant Freshour's card from her billfold and dialed his number.

After a short wait, Lieutenant Freshour came on the line. "This is Jeagan Christensen, Lieutenant. Have you talked with Isabel Lloyd this afternoon?"

"Yes," he said, his tone somewhat impatient. "I talked to her around noon, and I tried to call you at the hotel."

"Sorry, I…uh…took a drive," Jeagan said. "How was she?"

"She sounded a little groggy, but otherwise, she said she was okay."

"Groggy doesn't surprise me. At least she's alive," Jeagan said. "What exactly did she say to you?"

"Only that she was very tired."

"Listen, Lieutenant. I'm in Dovington and I'm really worried about her."

"What are you doing in Dovington?"

"This is where Isabel gave birth to her baby in 1945. She told me the baby was stillborn. But, I think I've found proof that the baby was alive."

"What does that have to do with now?" the lieutenant had that give-it-up tone in his voice.

"Remember I told you that Isabel's sister said something about having to take care of something now?"

"Yes. I remember you saying that."

"Well, I think when I came to Memphis and stirred up the past, Agnes got scared. It appears to me that she might have been afraid I'd uncovered what I did."

Lieutenant Freshour sighed. "Do you know for certain that Isabel's baby was alive at birth?"

"Well...not exactly. There's no record of Isabel ever giving birth to a baby here in April of 1945. But, I believe her father admitted her to the hospital under a false name, and the baby was given the first name of his father—Alan, which is what Isabel said she would have named him had he lived."

Lieutenant Freshour's voice rose slightly. "Miss Christensen...Jeagan, that doesn't prove anything. What was the name of the mother?"

"Well," Jeagan said hesitantly as doubts clouded her thinking. "The records show that her name was Jane Koehler, but I'm sure the mother was Isabel. The records show that she was from Memphis."

"That *still* doesn't prove anything." The lieutenant paused, as if collecting his patience. "Look, Miss Christensen. I know you're concerned about your friend and mean well, but you have no real basis for your suspicions."

"I know I don't have anything concrete, but I'm sure I'm right," she said. "I need to see Isabel again and find out if her father signed her in as Jane Koehler when she was sent here to have her baby."

"I don't think that's a good idea," the lieutenant said. "The family appears to be tired of you making a nuisance of yourself. If you keep trying to contact Isabel, they might file harassment charges against you."

"If I don't keep pushing for the truth, I'm afraid her family will dispose of her before she finds out that her son was not stillborn."

"For your own good, I advise you to leave the woman alone," Lieutenant Freshour said firmly.

Jeagan tried to placate the lieutenant. "Okay. Point taken, Lieutenant. But, will you do one more thing for me, then I'll quit bothering you?"

"You're not bothering me," the lieutenant said, exasperation evident in his voice, "but I wish you would look clearly at what you're doing and saying. You've trespassed and now you've gotten information from a hospital that normally takes a release of liability form. I hope you didn't do anything dishonest to get the information?"

"No. Well...not really."

"Don't tell me. I don't want to know."

"Okay, but what I need you to do is check on the car accident Isabel had a couple of years ago. As a result of the accident, she's confined to a wheelchair. I have this feeling that it wasn't an accident."

"Okay...fine. If it will make you feel better and get you on your way back to Denver, I'll check it out. Give me the details."

Jeagan related the few details of the accident that she had, then added. "A friend of mine, Madison, I mean Darrell Hannah, who's a Memphis attorney, checked with a friend of his at the Memphis Police Department. Madi...Darrell said Sergeant Jim Hylton told him there wasn't anything suspicious about the wreck, but maybe you might see something in the file that Sergeant Hylton didn't."

Lieutenant Freshour's patience appeared to be wearing thin. "Look, Miss Christensen. I'm sure that if Sergeant Hylton didn't find anything suspicious about the accident, then I won't find anything either."

"Would you at least check? I can't help worrying about this. I want to make sure Isabel is safe, then I'll go back to Denver."

Lieutenant Freshour laughed. "Now, that sounds like a good idea."

Jeagan chose to ignore the remark.

"I'll see what I can do," Lieutenant Freshour said. "Where can I reach you?"

"I'm on my way back to Memphis. I should be back at the hotel by four o'clock. But, let me give you my cell phone number." After Jeagan disconnected, she started her car and pulled onto the highway.

*   *   *

Parked behind the gas station, he watched Jeagan pull out into traffic. He dialed the now-familiar number. "She appears to be on her way back to Memphis," he said into the phone. After he listened for a moment, he added. "I'm on my way back there now. I'll let you know what I find out."

Chapter Twenty

Jeagan drove along the black ribbon of highway that headed south toward Memphis. As she drove, she wondered about baby Alan. He had to be Isabel's son. Everything, including the name, fit so well. What had happened to him, Jeagan wondered? Most likely, he was at least alive at birth. Isabel needed to know that. Jeagan would try to get through to her when she reached the hotel. Surely the butler would at least let her talk to Isabel. If not, Jeagan was not sure what she could or would do.

She tried to relax and enjoy the white-blossomed dogwoods and bright pink azaleas scattered across the countryside. She rolled down the windows and let the warm spring air tousle her hair. But, she could not keep her mind off of Isabel and baby Alan.

Maybe Agnes knew about the baby. Maybe after their father died and left most of his estate to Isabel, Agnes tried to run Isabel off the road so she could inherit the entire estate, including what was left of the money. Or, maybe Agnes had hired someone to cause the accident. If left to die of natural causes, Isabel would in all likelihood leave the estate to Agnes anyway. But, maybe Agnes was greedy and wanted the money sooner rather than later.

Then there was the chance that she knew about baby Alan and wanted to make sure Isabel was out of the way before she somehow found out about him and left the estate to him. So many possibilities.

Maybe Jeagan should ask Madison what he considered the chances were of someone finding their child after fifty years. Baby Alan was most likely adopted and would probably be very hard to trace, but with extenuating circumstances, there might be a chance the records could be opened.

When Jeagan reached Memphis and drove into the Peabody parking garage, she knew what she would do. She would call Isabel and ask if she had used the pseudonym of Jane Koehler while confined in the hospital. Then, Jeagan would call Lieutenant Freshour to see if he had any additional information on the accident.

*   *   *

The Peabody garage was not crowded when Jeagan arrived. She found a spot on the first floor, got out, and locked her car. She crossed the sidewalk to the back entrance of the hotel. As she did, she spotted Edward Coffey. He was apparently waiting for his car at the valet parking stand. He waved. She smiled and headed toward him, wishing only to say hello and continue into the hotel.

She stepped onto the sidewalk. "Hi, Edward."

"Hi." Edward grinned as his eyes roamed over Jeagan's body. "You're looking great today. How about dinner tonight?"

Was Edward drooling again or was it only perspiration? Jeagan tried to sound polite. "Thank you, but no. I have plans for tonight and then I'm leaving tomorrow."

Edward appeared momentarily disappointed, then tried again. He looked at Jeagan with liquid eyes. "How about breakfast in the morning then?"

Obviously, Edward had forgotten that she might be a thief. Male hormones versus common sense. No contest in Edward's case. Jeagan made her voice sound firm. "Edward, I really can't. I have a few things I need to do before my flight tomorrow. Goodbye." Jeagan touched Edward's arm. "Take care of yourself."

"But..." Edward watched Jeagan's retreating back as she entered the hotel. His eyes turned hard and cold.

After Jeagan entered the hotel, she turned around to see if Edward was following her. She saw that he still stood there and looked toward the hotel. Then, her eyes moved to his car as the valet parked it at the curb. It was a brown Taurus. Stunned, Jeagan forgot to watch where she was going and ran into a wall.

She stepped back, tried to regain her balance and composure, and glanced outside to see Edward, his back to her, now talking on his cell phone. *I cannot wait to get away from this place,* she told herself.

When she turned and entered the lobby, she felt relieved to see Ken Rockwell in a conversation with one of the housekeeping crew. Seeing Rockwell made her remember the sandy-haired man. She had completely forgotten about him, and, thankfully, had not seen *him* today. Jeagan approached the Security Officer.

Rockwell turned toward Jeagan as she approached. "Oh, Miss Christensen. I've got some good news for you," he said, obviously pleased with himself.

"You've found the sandy-haired man?" Jeagan hoped this was the good news.

Rockwell's smile dissolved. "No. But, we have talked with all the hotel staff. The man is not registered here."

A touch of sarcasm in her voice, Jeagan said, "Well, I guess that's some progress."

"It's a start," Rockwell said and appeared to either ignore or not notice the sarcasm. "We've also got the man's description posted in all employee areas. Everyone is keeping an eye out for him and will call me immediately if he's spotted on the premises." Rockwell's chest puffed out as if to say he was in charge of the operation with all his troops following his direct orders.

Jeagan smiled and tried to sound sincere. "Thanks for all you've done. I feel safer now that you've put the whole hotel on alert." She appreciated the man's efforts, but did not feel confident that Ken Rockwell would locate the stalker. "I've got another problem now."

Rockwell's eyes brightened with interest. "Let's have a seat over here and I'll see what we can do about your problem."

Jeagan followed Rockwell and sat in a brown leather wingback across an end table from him. "Remember I said I thought the sandy-haired man followed me to Merle?"

Rockwell nodded. "Yes."

"When I saw him, or at least who I thought was him, he was sitting in a brown Taurus. But, outside a few minutes ago, I saw my neighbor in room 1006 get into a brown Taurus."

Rockwell looked puzzled and waved his hand in a rolling motion. "And?"

"*And*, he's been pestering me for the last couple of days." Jeagan was thoughtful for a moment. "In fact, he's been pestering me since the day after I first visited Isabel."

"So," Rockwell said, doubtful, "you think he registered here so he could spy on you?"

Jeagan sighed and ran her fingers through her hair. "I don't know what I think anymore. When you say it out loud, it sounds silly, but maybe the two men are friends and take turns using the brown Taurus to spy on me."

Rockwell's frown showed what he thought about that idea. "So, you're talking conspiracy here."

"No." Jeagan surveyed the lobby and tried to pull her thoughts together. "I don't know what I'm 'talking.' All I know is that one man is making a pest of himself and one man appears to be following me, and both men drive a brown Taurus."

"Did you get a license number off either car?"

"Well, no...I didn't think of that." As Rockwell's eyebrows arched, she raised her hands in mock surrender. "I know. I know I should have."

Rockwell nodded. "Do you know the man's name in room 1006?"

"Yes. It's Edward Coffey. He's some kind of insurance salesman in town for a meeting, so he says."

Rockwell wrote the name in his book. "I'll check him out."

"Thanks." Jeagan touched Rockwell's hand. "I really do appreciate your help."

Ken Rockwell smiled and stood. "That's what I'm here for. Now, don't you worry. I have my people keeping an eye out for you. No one will bother you as long as you're in this hotel."

"That's certainly reassuring." She looked at her watch. "Well, I guess I better get up to my room and get ready for dinner."

"Let me know if you need anything. We'll be close by," Rockwell said.

As she headed for the elevator, Jeagan told herself that she had less than twenty-four hours to stay in Memphis and had to be alert. Tonight she would be with Madison, so at least she would not be alone.

When she returned to her room, she noticed that the message light was not lit and her cell phone had not rung. She dropped her handbag on the dresser and sat on the bed. Then, she dialed information and tried to get a number for Isabel Lloyd in Oxford. The information operator informed Jeagan that the number was unlisted. Jeagan frowned. Unfortunately, that was what she expected.

There must be a way to reach Isabel, she thought, but she had no idea how. She stretched out across the bed on her stomach and rested her head on her folded arms. Maybe the lieutenant would give her Isabel's number if she asked. Not very likely, she thought. He wanted her to leave Isabel alone. And, since he had not called, apparently he had found out nothing new about Isabel's accident.

Use your brain, your common sense, Jeagan told herself. After a few moments, she snapped her fingers. She pulled herself up and checked the number she had for Isabel's home. Possibly the maid would give her the number in Oxford, if Agnes had not left instructions not to give the number out. Jeagan grabbed the phone and dialed the number.

"Lloyd residence," the pleasant, quiet voice said. Jeagan could tell that it was the same person, the maid, who had answered the phone the day before.

"Yes. Hello. I'm a friend of Isabel's—Jeagan Christensen? I called yesterday?"

"Yes, ma'am?" the maid said.

"I'm trying to reach Isabel at her home in Oxford, and I seem to have misplaced the number. Could you give it to me?"

The maid hesitated. "Well, I guess it would be all right if you're a friend of hers. What did you say your name was?"

Hopeful, Jeagan said, "Jeagan Christensen. I called last night when Isabel did not make the opera performance."

"Oh, yes. I remember. All right, Miz Christensen." The maid recited the number, which Jeagan scrawled in her daytimer.

Jeagan breathed a sigh of relief, thanked the maid, disconnected, and then dialed the number in Oxford, Mississippi.

"Lloyd residence." Jeagan recognized the voice of Williams, the butler.

With an attempt at a southern accent, Jeagan said, "I'd like to speak with Isabel, please."

"Who's calling, please?" Williams asked.

Jeagan's mind raced. "I'm Phoebe Reynolds from the Memphis Opera Society."

"Miss Isabel is resting now. I'll be glad to have her call you if you'll leave your number, Miss Reynolds."

Jeagan's mind went blank. "I—I'm leaving the office for the afternoon. I'll try her later." She disconnected. It was useless to try to reach Isabel this way. The butler would probably not let her through, and Jeagan could never leave her number.

Jeagan walked over to the window and pulled the sheers aside. She looked out over the city. At the rate I'm going, I'll never be able to get through to Isabel before my flight tomorrow, Jeagan thought. No, she could not leave until she talked to Isabel again and knew that she was safe—and found out if she had registered as Jane Koehler at the sanitarium in Dovington. Jeagan checked the time. Soon she would have to dress for dinner, but first...She went back to the nightstand, picked up the phone, and dialed Isabel's home again.

"Lloyd residence," the maid said when she answered.

"Uh...yes...this is Jeagan Christensen again."

"Yes, ma'am?" the maid said expectantly.

"I was wondering if you could give me Isabel's address in Oxford. I'll...uh...be in Oxford tomorrow and would like to stop in and see her."

"I'm sorry Miz Christensen," the maid hesitated as if unsure how to continue, "but Miz Harraway just called and asked if she had received any calls. When I told her you had called for Miz Isabel, Miz Harraway told me not to give you any more information about Miz Isabel."

"Oh, I see," Jeagan said and she did see—very clearly. Agnes Harraway would block all her attempts to contact Isabel. "Well, thank you anyway." Jeagan hung up the phone.

The one thing Isabel had going for her now, Jeagan realized, was that the police had checked on her twice since she had been in Oxford. Hopefully, Agnes would not attempt to hurt Isabel with all the attention she was receiving.

As she changed into her jungle print dress for dinner, Jeagan heard a beeping sound. It sounded like her...Oh, no. She had forgotten to charge the battery for her cell phone. It was useless to her now. It would have to be recharged. She pulled out the charger and placed the phone on it.

*   *   *

At five o'clock, Jeagan entered the hotel lobby and crossed to a celery-colored, overstuffed sofa to wait for Madison. When he had not arrived by ten after five, she began to worry. But, minutes later he strode through the back doors of the hotel, dressed in a crisp white shirt with the sleeves rolled up and the neck unbuttoned, red paisley tie—loosened, and gray dress slacks.

"I'm sorry to be so late," Madison said. "My client wanted to talk after the hearing. I told him I had another appointment, but I guess he figured since he had driven in from Tupelo for the hearing that my time was his time. I finally was able to get away from him with a promise that I would meet him for breakfast tomorrow morning in Tupelo." He plopped into a plump armchair.

Jeagan attempted a smile. "I'm sorry to take you away from your client, Madison. We could have gone to dinner a little later."

"No way," Madison said. "You're leaving tomorrow and Dan will be still be around long after you're gone. By the way, you look great," he added.

Jeagan grinned. "Thanks, Madison. So do you."

Madison leaned over and touched Jeagan's hand, which rested on the arm of her chair. "Are you all right? You look upset."

Jeagan moved her hand involuntarily. Madison appeared not to notice.

"I'm still worried about Isabel," she said. "I can't get through to her in Oxford because they're screening her calls. I really need to talk to her about something that I found out today."

Madison stifled a sigh. A look of annoyance crossed his face. "Why can't you quit worrying about her? I thought you said you had talked to a police lieutenant who had checked on her for you?"

"I did and he did, but after what I found out today...," Jeagan said.

Madison crossed his arms and settled back into the armchair with a look of resignation on his face. "Okay. So tell me, what did you find out today?"

"I think I've found out that Isabel's son was alive at birth—not stillborn. And, I think her sister wants to get rid of her before she finds out and changes her will."

Madison sat forward. "Good Lord, Jeagan. Do you know for sure that her son was alive at birth?"

Jeagan shifted in her chair. "Well, no, I'm not one hundred percent positive, but..."

"Okay, then," Madison's forehead wrinkled in a frown. "Until you know for sure, you probably shouldn't go around accusing people of plotting murder."

"But…," Jeagan began.

Madison reached over and squeezed Jeagan's hand. "I know you mean well, but all these plots and subplots. Look, you've told Isabel what you came to tell her. Yes, maybe she's upset now, but I'm sure she'll get over it soon. Anyway, a weekend at her country house in the woods and she'll probably be fine by Monday."

"Maybe you're right, but if baby Alan did live…," Jeagan said.

"Have you told that police lieutenant what you think you found?" Madison asked.

Jeagan shrugged. "I tried, but he basically told me to butt out and go home."

Madison grinned. "Sounds like good advice to me."

"I know, Madison, but I can't go home until I talk to Isabel one more time. I need to ask her if her father checked her into the sanitarium under a different name—Jane Koehler."

Madison appeared thoughtful. "Well, since you've already ruined our fun evening…"

Jeagan momentarily forgot Isabel. "Oh, Madison, I'm sorry. We can still go to Beale Street if you want to. I promise I'll try to have a good time."

Madison shook his head and laughed. "I find that hard to believe." He placed his hands on the arms of the chair and pushed himself to his feet. "I tell you what, why don't we drive down to Oxford to see your Isabel. The butler can't turn us away if she's there. You can talk to her and tell her what you've found out, and then we can still catch a late dinner somewhere. Oxford is only a little over an hour away."

"I'd hate to ask you to do that," Jeagan said and looked up at Madison. "Besides, I don't even know her address."

"I can probably fix that." He pulled out a pen and picked up his cocktail napkin.

"How can you get her address when the information operator told me her number was unlisted?"

"Don't worry. I have my sources. I'll be right back. Why don't you order drinks for us while I go find a phone? Make mine mineral water, since I'm driving."

"Thanks, Madison. I owe you—big time."

Madison patted Jeagan's shoulder. "And, I intend to collect by overstaying my welcome when I come out to Denver to ski."

Jeagan laughed. "It's a deal." She relaxed as Madison crossed the lobby toward the pay phones. She looked around for a waitress. When she found one, she motioned her over and placed her order. Then, she sat back in her chair to wait for Madison. Hopefuly, he would be able to get Isabel's address.

Jeagan glanced around the lobby. As she did, she noticed that Madison had left his cell phone on the coffee table in front of them. She wondered why he had not used it to make the call. Maybe, like her, she thought, he did not use it unless he had to.

Soon, the waitress returned with their drinks. Jeagan signed the ticket and sipped her wine. Minutes later, Madison returned. He grinned and dangled his napkin in front of her. "Well, here's the address."

"Tell me how you found it," Jeagan teased.

"Never," said Madison. He picked up his glass of mineral water. After a long drink, he said, "I'm ready if you are."

"I'm ready," she said and took a last sip of her wine. She left with Madison out the back entrance of the hotel.

He fished in his shirt pocket for his parking ticket and handed it to the valet. Several minutes later, the valet parked a black Porsche in front of them.

"A Porsche no less," Jeagan said. "I'm impressed."

"Good," said Madison. The valet stepped out of the car and then came around to the passenger side to open the door for Jeagan. When she was inside, Madison tipped the valet and moved around the car and climbed behind the wheel. "Okay to put the top down?"

Jeagan smiled and nodded. "Absolutely. My hair looks better windblown."

* * *

As Jeagan and Madison drove out of the parking lot, Ken Rockwell, who led a sandy-haired man by the arm, walked into his office. "Sit down," he ordered. Rockwell dialed Jeagan's room, but there was no answer.

The sandy-haired man sat in a worn armchair, directly in front of the Security Officer, with his arms folded across his chest. A smug look settled on his rugged, tanned face as he leaned back in his chair.

Rockwell replaced the receiver. "Okay," he said, "Who are you and why have you been stalking Jeagan Christensen?"

"My name is Roger Sanderlin." The sandy-haired man sat forward and pulled out his Colorado driver's license, which he handed to Rockwell. "I'm a private investigator, and I haven't been stalking Jeagan. I've been keeping an eye on her for her dad."

"Her dad!" Surprise, as well as disappointment, spread like a wave over Rockwell's face.

"That's right," Roger said. He replaced his driver's license in his wallet. "Jeagan left Denver in a huff after an argument with her dad. He felt bad about the argument and sent me to make sure she didn't get herself into trouble."

"So, you've been following her around town?" Rockwell asked.

"Yes. I followed her around Memphis for a couple of days, then to Merle, Arkansas on Wednesday and today to Dovington, Tennessee. She's been doing a lot of prying and I'm afraid she's going to get herself into real trouble. So far, she's guilty of breaking and entering, trespassing, and obtaining medical information without a written consent."

"How do you know all that?" Rockwell asked.

"It's my job. I told you I'm a private investigator." Roger's tanned face broke into a boyish grin.

"Well," Rockwell said, as his disappointment deepened the lines around his mouth, "I guess she'll be glad to hear that you aren't a stalker...and so will Lieutenant Freshour."

Rockwell reached for the phone and pulled out Lieutenant Freshour's card. He dialed the number of the East Precinct. When the lieutenant came on the line, he said, "This is Ken Rockwell at the Peabody. I have the man who has been following Jeagan Christensen in my office."

"Good work, Rockwell," Lieutenant Freshour said. "What does the man have to say?"

"Well, Lieutenant," Rockwell leaned back in his chair and scratched his head. "He says that Jeagan's dad hired him to watch out for her."

Lieutenant Freshour let out a laugh that made Rockwell momentarily jerk the phone away from his ear.

Roger could hear the lieutenant through the phone. He smothered a grin.

"That's a kick," Lieutenant Freshour said when the laughter subsided. "No wonder Isabel said no one who fit his description worked for her. Does Jeagan know yet?"

"Well, no," Rockwell said, not finding the situation humorous. "I've tried her room, but there's no answer."

"I saw her in the lobby with that attorney friend of hers before you snagged me on the mezzanine," Roger said.

Rockwell repeated what Roger said to the lieutenant.

Lieutenant Freshour was quiet for a moment. "I've also been trying to reach Jeagan. Is that attorney friend of hers named Darrell Hannah by any chance?"

"I'm not good as a middle man," Rockwell said and pressed the speaker button on the phone. "He wants to talk to you."

"Yes, Lieutenant?" Roger said, as he leaned forward.

Lieutenant Freshour repeated the question. "Do you know the name of her attorney friend?"

"His name is Darrell Hannah, and he works for..."

"That's what I was afraid of."

Roger stiffened. "Why's that?"

"She asked me to check into a car accident that Isabel was involved in. Jeagan said she had her friend, Hannah, check with his buddy, a Sergeant Jim Hylton at the Memphis Police Department."

"And?" Roger said.

"*And,* first there *is* no Sergeant Jim Hylton at the Memphis Police Department, and second, Darrell Hannah is listed as the only witness to the accident."

Roger looked puzzled. "That doesn't make any sense."

"I know it doesn't, but there it is." The lieutenant hesitated, then said, "I'm on my way over. That young lady may have known what she was talking about all along." The sound of the lieutenant grabbing his car keys could be heard through the phone. "Rockwell?"

Rockwell straightened in his chair. "I'm here."

"Check with your staff to see if anybody knows where Jeagan and Hannah went. I'll be there in ten minutes."

"Will do." Ken Rockwell looked at Roger. "Want to help?"

"Let's go." Roger stood.

"By the way, do you know a guy named Edward Coffey?" Rockwell asked as he opened the office door.

Roger shook his head. "No, I don't know him, but I've seen him sniffing around Jeagan, so I checked on him. He's an insurance salesman, married, but seems to like the ladies. I've seen him hit on two or three gals over the last few days."

"Yeah. I checked him out for Jeagan. She thought you two were in cahoots and taking turns following her."

"Not likely. That guy's a sleaze," Roger said as they walked down the hall.

Rockwell made a note in his little notebook. "I'll think I'll have a talk with Mr. Edward Coffey." He replaced the notebook in his pocket. "Okay, where did you see Jeagan last?" Rockwell asked as they entered the lobby.

"Like I said," Roger answered, "she was here in the lobby having a drink with Hannah when you grabbed me."

Rockwell slapped Roger on the shoulder. "Sorry about that. Just doing my job."

"That's okay," Roger said. "I have no idea where they went when they left, but they seemed to be in a hurry to get there. I would have followed them if…"

"I know, I know." Rockwell shrugged his shoulders. "My timing was not too good." He looked around the lobby. "Maybe one of the other folks out here might have overheard them." More than thirty people sat around the lobby in groups, drinking and talking. "Where were they sitting?"

"Over by the piano." Roger pointed to a softly lit seating area close to the grand piano. Strains of "Think of Me" floated across the lobby.

"Okay, I'll start over there and see if I can find out anything," Rockwell said. "You take the other side of the lobby."

Ken Rockwell questioned three groups close to the piano. One woman remembered seeing Jeagan and Madison, but had paid no attention to their conversation.

Roger questioned people on the other side of the lobby. Two men remembered seeing Jeagan and Madison, but had not been close enough to hear their conversation. About to give up, Roger questioned a man who came from the men's room.

"Excuse me?" Roger said.

The tall, gray-haired man, impeccably dressed in a navy suit and yellow print tie, stopped to acknowledge Roger. "What can I do for you?"

"I'm trying to find anyone who remembers seeing a black man, thirtyish, medium height, dressed in a white dress shirt and gray slacks who was with a young white woman dressed in a jungle-type print outfit?"

The man paused for a moment to think. "I don't remember the woman, but I believe I saw the man back here. He was talking on the phone."

Roger was hopeful. "Did you overhear his conversation?"

"Just a few words. He seemed agitated. He said something about bringing her there."

"Bringing her there…? Did you happen to catch where *there* was?"

"No." The man shook his head. "Sorry."

Roger thanked the man and headed back to the front desk where Rockwell stood talking to Lieutenant Freshour.

"This is Roger Sanderlin, Lieutenant," Ken Rockwell said as Roger approached. Roger and Lieutenant Freshour shook hands. "Anybody know anything?" Rockwell asked.

"One guy overheard Hannah tell somebody over the phone that he was 'bringing her there,'" Roger said.

Ken Rockwell frowned. "That doesn't sound good. Don't guess you know where there is?"

Roger shook his head. "Not a clue."

"I think I do," Lieutenant Freshour said. Roger and Ken Rockwell both looked at the lieutenant.

"She's asked me to check on Isabel Lloyd twice today." He hesitated, thinking. "If Hannah was involved in the accident last year, he may be involved somehow with Agnes Harraway, Isabel's sister. Maybe Hannah's her attorney and she promised him part of the estate if he helped clear the way for her to inherit."

"Inherit seems to be the word of the day," Roger said.

"That's right," Lieutenant Freshour said. He thought for a moment. "If Jeagan was right about the baby being alive at birth and…if she told Hannah about the baby…"

"Then," Roger picked up the train of thought, "Hannah could be taking Jeagan to Agnes—or maybe to where both women are and…"

Lieutenant Freshour pulled a piece of paper and his cell phone out of his pocket. "Let's go. Thanks for your help, Rockwell."

"Anytime," Rockwell said. If only he could join in the action. "Good luck." He sighed and looked around the lobby. Guests stared at him with questioning looks on their faces. He smiled and stood taller. Surely they realized that with him on the job, they were safe. Edward Coffey, he remembered and frowned. I think I'll have a talk with that guy. Rockwell headed for his office.

The lieutenant strode toward the front of the hotel. He checked the piece of paper and dialed a number.

"Do you know where he took Jeagan?" Roger said, as he caught up with the lieutenant.

"Not yet, but I will in a minute."

After three rings, the phone was answered. "Harraway residence."

"This is Lieutenant Freshour of the Memphis Police Department. I need to speak with Agnes Harraway."

Her voice shaky, the maid said, "I—I'm sorry, Lieutenant. Miz Harraway is at the Oxford house."

"Get me the address of the Oxford house—and hurry."

After the lieutenant wrote down the address, he said, "I've got it. Just pray we're not too late."

"Shouldn't you get the local police involved?" Roger said. He pushed open the door to the street.

"I'm doing that right now." Lieutenant Freshour dialed a number on his cell phone. When they were inside his car, he flipped on the siren and jerked the car out into traffic. Cars that approached from behind screeched to a stop to let him pass. The patrol car screamed down Union toward the expressway. Lieutenant Freshour dug in his coat pocket, pulled out another slip of paper, and handed it to Roger. "Here's Jeagan's cell phone number. Try to reach her."

Roger tried to read the number as he bounced around in the patrol car. When the number was entered in his cell phone, he could barely hear the ring of Jeagan's cell phone above the wail of the siren. He stuck his finger in his other ear. After ten rings, he gave up.

Chapter Twenty-One

The cool air whipped Jeagan's hair across her face on the drive to Oxford. She looked over at Madison. He seemed preoccupied and had not said a word for the last fifteen minutes. But, with the top down and jazz blaring from the high-power stereo system, conversation would have been virtually impossible anyway. Still an uneasy feeling made her shudder. Something tugged at the back of her mind—something Madison had said earlier, but she could not remember what it was.

* * *

"Well, it looks like you're going to have visitors," Agnes Harraway said. She walked up beside Isabel, who sat in a white wicker chair in the flower garden of her Oxford home and idly picked dead blooms off one of the pale pink azalea bushes that surrounded the flagstone terrace.

Isabel looked up at Agnes. She could only see Agnes' dark outline against the afternoon sun. "Who?"

Agnes perched on a white wicker chair opposite Isabel. "Madison Hannah and that nosey girl from Denver," she said, her voice cool.

Isabel vaguely remembered the name Madison from somewhere in her past. "I can't believe you'd allow Jeagan to come here, when you brought me here to keep me away from her."

Agnes laughed, but her eyes showed no mirth. "She has something to tell you, I believe." Agnes rose from her chair and left Isabel to think about what else Jeagan could possibly have to tell her.

Did Jeagan know Isabel was a prisoner in her own house, she wondered. Certainly, Jeagan had good intentions, but Isabel wished Jeagan had never come to Memphis. She had reopened old wounds and told Isabel that her father was a murderer. As a

142

result, her life had been a nightmare for the past few days. As soon as Isabel told Agnes what Jeagan knew about Alan's murder, Agnes and Williams had packed Isabel off to Oxford. What difference it could make to Agnes after all these years, Isabel could not imagine.

Isabel knew her sister resented the fact that their father had left most of his estate to her. And, now, she was afraid of her sister. Agnes had given her tranquilizers three times a day since she arrived, with the excuse that Isabel had received a nasty shock at the news of her late fiancé's murder.

The last two times Agnes had tried to give her tablets, Isabel had pretended to take them, but had managed to drop both into her teacup at lunch and dinner as she took a sip. The tablet soon dissolved and Isabel had drunk only water after that. She had maintained the appearance of being calm and somewhat groggy all day, although her mind was alert.

Isabel wished Lieutenant Freshour would call again. She wondered if the incorrect things she had told him had been relayed to Jeagan and if that was the reason she was on her way to Oxford. Even so, if the lieutenant would just keep checking on Isabel, Agnes might take Isabel back to Memphis, but Jeagan coming to Oxford did not sound like a good idea. They were too far from Memphis and the police. And, who was Madison? Isabel tried to remember where she had heard that name but could not.

*　*　*

As they passed through the town of Oxford, Jeagan enjoyed seeing the old, established college community, lush with mature trees, rolling hills, and bright spring flowers. The town was graced with well-preserved, two-story, columned homes that looked to have been built around the turn of the century. They passed the University of Mississippi, or Ole Miss as it was known, with hundreds of fully mature oaks and maples and pines that shaded the stately stone buildings of the various colleges.

Part of Jeagan wished she had the time to be a tourist and roam the town. She would like to visit William Faulkner's estate and drive by John Grisham's home. Still, the other part of her wanted to reach Isabel as soon as possible and see for herself that she was all right.

Madison, still silent, seemed to know exactly where he was going. Jeagan noticed that he did not even consult a map or street signs. Finally, after driving through town, they entered a long, tree-lined country lane with only a few large homes set far back from the road in park-like settings at quarter-mile intervals. Ten minutes later, they came on an eight-foot, gray stone wall with a black wrought-iron gate. Madison pressed a button at the entrance and a voice came over the speaker.

"Yes?"

"It's Madison."

Jeagan's mouth dropped open as the gate swung inward. Madison drove up the tree-lined driveway to a white, two-story, columned house that looked like something out of *Gone with the Wind.* Chills crept up her spine as they passed massive magnolia, oak, and mimosa trees spread across the lush, expansive front lawn.

"What's going on, Madison?" Jeagan asked. She hugged herself to keep from shaking.

Madison did not answer. He passed the circular gravel drive in front and drove around to the back of the house where he parked near the garage. As soon as he stopped the car, Agnes Harraway stepped out from the large screened porch. Her right hand inside the pocket of her black linen slacks, she walked over to the passenger side of the car and pulled open the door.

"How nice to see you again, Miss Christensen," Agnes said, her voice cold and brittle.

Confused and now a little scared, Jeagan said, "What's going on? How did you know we were coming here?"

Agnes smiled, "Madison and I don't have many secrets. He's told me all about what you've been doing the last few days. You've been a nosey little bitch, haven't you?" Agnes pulled a

.32 caliber handgun from her pocket and pointed it at Jeagan. "Get out of the car."

Numb with rising fear, Jeagan turned to Madison for help. He did not look at her. He simply got out of the car and entered the house.

Agnes held Jeagan securely by the arm as she stepped out of the car and followed Madison. Once inside, Agnes led Jeagan through an airy, yellow, country kitchen and through the formal dining room into a bright family room with sunny west windows.

Jeagan saw Isabel seated in her wheelchair near a ten-foot, red brick fireplace—now cold and dark.

Isabel appeared groggy, but she smiled sadly when she saw Jeagan.

Relieved to see Isabel, Jeagan wrenched her arm from Agnes' grip and went to Isabel's side.

"Are you all right?" Jeagan said as she took one of Isabel's hands and knelt in front of her on the green floral carpet.

Isabel smoothed Jeagan's hair back from her face.

A sharp pain shot through Jeagan's heart as a fleeting memory of her mother doing the same thing many times ran through her mind.

"I'm fine, dear." Isabel's sad, gray eyes betrayed her words.

Jeagan stood and faced Agnes. "How did you know we were coming here, and how do you know Madison?"

Madison walked over to a picture window that overlooked the terrace and garden beyond. His back to Jeagan, he still said nothing.

Agnes glanced at Madison. "Well, Madison, will you tell her or do I have to?"

Madison waved his hand in the air, but did not turn around.

Agnes shrugged. "Have it your way. Leave it to me like everything else." Agnes sat on the chintz sofa and ran her hand over the fabric. "I never liked this furniture," she said, as if to herself. "I think I'll get rid of it and redecorate." She glared at Jeagan and Isabel, dark hatred in her eyes. "You have no one to blame but yourself, Jeagan Christensen. You should have stayed in Colorado and kept out of our business."

Jeagan's knees gave way and she sat on the floor beside Isabel, still holding her hand. She looked up at Isabel's tear-filled eyes.

"Then it's true," Jeagan said, her suspicions confirmed. "You are after Isabel's money. You want to get rid of her so you can inherit the estate. You tried to have her killed in that car accident, didn't you?"

Agnes inspected the pear-shaped diamond-and-platinum wedding ring on her right hand. At least she had been able to hang onto that after her nasty divorce. There were not many assets left to split after her worthless husband squandered their savings at the casinos in Tunica. "Madison bungled that one pretty badly, didn't you, Madison?" she said. Madison never moved.

Jeagan's head snapped toward Madison. "Madison!"

"Yes, dear...Madison," Agnes said. "He tried to dispose of Isabel, but she managed to survive the accident. We had decided to leave her alone after that and let her die of natural causes. That is, until you made your unwelcome appearance."

"I only came here to try to help Isabel," Jeagan said. "I thought that if I could prove her fiancé was killed, then she could rest a little easier knowing what had happened to him." Jeagan's eyes pleaded for understanding. "I meant no harm to anyone."

Madison turned from the window. His emotions were on the surface. "Why couldn't you let it go, Jeagan? I really liked you and wanted to get to know you better."

"What have I done that's so awful? Isabel's father is dead. The murder happened fifty years ago. What's so terrible about her knowing the truth?"

Madison's eyes hardened. "Tell Isabel what you did today."

Jeagan slowly turned to Isabel. She took both of Isabel's hands. "Did your father use a false name for you when he signed you in to the sanitarium to have your baby?"

Isabel nodded and hung her head. "He was afraid someone would find out that I had disgraced my family, so he signed me in as Jane Koehler."

Jeagan felt as if someone had poured ice water down her back. She squeezed Isabel's hands. "I thought so. Isabel, your son was not stillborn. Alan was alive at birth."

Isabel's head shot up. "Alive? Alan wasn't stillborn?"

"No. He wasn't," Agnes said with a sigh. "Father gave him up for adoption and told you he was dead."

"How could he do that to me?" Isabel demanded, trembling.

"I was only nine at the time and had no idea what he did, but you know as well as I do what made him do it—pride. Family pride. He could never have faced his friends again if you had disgraced him by bringing home an illegitimate child."

An inner light lit Isabel's eyes; her anger subsided. "Then Alan might still be alive."

"Exactly," Agnes said.

Slowly, the light disappeared from Isabel's eyes. "Then, that's it. You wanted to make sure you got me out of the way before I found out that I have a son who could be my heir."

"Damn you, Jeagan!" Madison left the house and slammed the back door behind him.

Jeagan turned toward Agnes. "No harm has been done to anyone, Agnes. Why can't you just let it go?"

"Because your digging around has got the police nipping at our heels. You've had that police lieutenant calling us and sooner or later, he's going to dig out that accident report and realize that Madison, who is almost a member of the family by the way, was involved in the accident that almost killed Isabel."

"What do you mean by 'member of the family'?" Jeagan asked.

Williams, the butler, entered the room, as if he had waited for his introduction. "Madison is my nephew."

Jeagan sank to the floor again. "No. This can't be true." She focused on Agnes. "How can you people be so cruel?"

Agnes laughed. "That's not the half of it." She stood and moved toward the window and looked out at Madison, who was slumped on the wicker lounge chair. She turned toward Jeagan. "Williams was there the night our dear father killed Alan. He helped to dispose of Alan's body."

The color drained from Isabel's face. "Good Lord! How could you have done such a thing? We grew up together, Thomas."

"Thomas?" Jeagan said. "I thought your name was Williams." Jeagan turned her head toward the butler.

"It is. Thomas Williams."

"You!" Jeagan's voice choked in her throat. "It was you."

Thomas Williams' eyes narrowed to black slits and he nodded his head. "Yes," he said. "I was there and so were you. I saw you, but you disappeared before I could reach you. I always wondered why you didn't go to the police."

"I...I...," Jeagan began.

"Then," the butler continued, "I recognized you the minute I opened the door when you came around asking for Isabel. I don't know how you managed it since you look the same as you did fifty years ago, but it was you, unless it was your mother I saw fifty years ago."

"Oh, my God!" Jeagan trembled all over. "I was actually there. I actually witnessed the murder." Sobs wracked her body as she buried her head in Isabel's lap. Isabel protectively covered Jeagan's head.

Agnes walked out the back door and spoke to Madison. He shook his head and did not look up at her. "You coward!" she yelled and marched back into the house. The screen door slammed behind her. "It's up to you and me," she said to Williams.

Williams went into the kitchen and returned momentarily with silver duct tape. He ripped off a large piece. Jeagan jumped at the tearing sound. She raised her head and looked up as Williams grabbed her hands and pulled them behind her back. He wound tape around them. "What are you doing?" she cried.

148

"Don't worry about it," he mumbled. "You'll know soon enough."

Williams tore off another piece of tape and slapped it across her mouth. Jeagan tried to control herself. Her heart pounded in her ears as terror filled her very soul. She turned to look out the back windows to see if Madison was still there. He was their only hope. If he did not help them, no one would. She had been so wrong about him. How could she have not seen through him?

Williams ripped more tape and bound Isabel's hands together and then wrapped tape across her mouth.

"Let's get them out to the van," Agnes said.

Williams nodded. He grabbed the handles of Isabel's wheelchair and pushed her toward the kitchen.

Agnes pulled Jeagan from the floor and pushed her after Williams. Once outside, Jeagan looked toward Madison, who was bent forward with his head in his hands. "Madison!" Jeagan screamed through the tape.

"Don't waste your time," Agnes said and jammed the gun in Jeagan's back as she steered her toward the garage. "Madison won't help you."

In the garage, Williams lifted Isabel's slight body into the back seat of the van and strapped her in. Her muffled sobs and tear-filled eyes pleaded for him to let her go. He ignored her pleas and calmly placed her wheelchair in the back.

Agnes pushed Jeagan, who kicked and struggled, into the van beside Isabel. Agnes slapped Jeagan hard across the face and held her while Williams bound her feet with the duct tape and strapped her in. Williams pulled the door closed and climbed behind the wheel. Agnes got into her red Cadillac Eldorado that was parked next to the white van.

"I'll follow you," Agnes said through the open window.

Williams nodded and backed out of the garage. He headed around the side of the house and down the driveway.

Tears stung Jeagan's eyes and slipped down over the raw handprint on her cheek. She wiped at the tears with her shoulder so she could see Madison out the window. He had not moved.

149

He still sat on the lounge chair with his head in his hands. He's useless, she thought. He cares too much to participate in this but too little to stop it.

She turned toward Isabel. Isabel was in shock—her eyes glazed and unfocused.

"I'm sorry, dad," Jeagan's mind cried. "I love you. I never meant to hurt you. I only wanted to pry you out of your self-pity and make you care about me for a change." A cold terror gripped Jeagan's body. When she realized she would never see her dad again, especially since they had parted on bad terms, she forced her mind to focus on what she could do to stop Agnes and Williams. She could not let them kill Isabel and her.

Williams slowly drove down the country road behind the estate that was bordered by rolling pastures where black cattle leisurely grazed. Jeagan's mind raced for some way of escape. After about a mile, the road seemed to dead end into water. Williams stopped at the water's edge, got out of the van, and walked back to wait for Agnes, who soon pulled in behind him.

Jeagan searched for something sharp inside the van. She spotted a piece of metal that stuck out of the floor that held the seat belt in place. The edge looked rough enough that it might eventually wear a hole in the tape if Jeagan could reach it. She stretched her bound hands around to the seatbelt fastener and pressed the button to unlatch it. When it popped open, she shifted her body toward the floor, then angled it so that she could work her wrists against the metal. The tape tightened as she sawed it against the rough edge.

Suddenly, the back door of the van swung open. Williams reached in, ripped the tape off Jeagan's feet, and roughly pushed her into the passenger seat in the front. She struck out at him with her elbows and feet, but Agnes grabbed her arms as Williams strapped Jeagan in. Next, Williams moved Isabel to the driver's seat and strapped her in.

Jeagan struggled to free herself, but suddenly her world turned black. The last things she remembered were bright, sparkling lights and a sharp pain in the back of her head.

Agnes jerked the tape off Jeagan's hands and mouth and then closed the van door.

Williams waved his hand in front of Isabel's face. She did not blink. He pulled the tape off her hands and mouth. He started the van and put it into drive.

*　*　*

Madison could not move. How had he sunk so deep into the mire of deceit and murder? Money, he thought. When Agnes had tempted him with three hundred thousand dollars to help her get rid of Isabel, Madison could not resist. After all, he had rationalized, Isabel was close to seventy and would not live much longer anyway. What had he been thinking? Now, a beautiful young woman, who had tried to give Isabel some peace of mind, was involved in this horrible mess and was about to lose her life along with Isabel. But, what could Madison do? If Jeagan were allowed to live, she would talk to the police and Madison's career and life would be over. Maybe drowning would not be so bad for the two women. He had heard that if you kept swallowing the water…

Suddenly the high-pitched whine of sirens filled the air. Madison sprang from his chair and ran to the side of the house. He looked down the drive. Seconds later, a patrol car crashed through the wrought-iron gate and screamed up the driveway. Another car followed close behind. Madison turned and ran for the woods behind the house.

Roger spotted Madison at the side of the house and was the first to jump out of the car. "There's Hannah!" he shouted and raced after him. As he rounded the house, he saw Madison near the edge of the woods. Roger cleared a three-foot, split-rail fence and raced after Madison. Within moments, he caught him and threw his weight at him. Both men tumbled to the ground. Roger pulled himself to his knees and grabbed Madison, who lay on his face, stunned from the fall.

Roger jerked Madison over on his back and pulled him up by his shirt collar. "Where is she?" Roger yelled.

As he spit dirt and grass out of his mouth, Madison realized it was over. "They took them to the lake down the road behind the house," he mumbled.

Roger threw Madison back on the ground and ran toward the house. When Roger neared the back porch, Lieutenant Freshour came out the screen door with two Oxford deputy sheriffs. "Nobody's inside."

Roger ran for the car. "They took them down to the lake behind the house. Let's go!"

The lieutenant and one of the deputies headed for their cars, while another deputy drew his gun and headed toward Madison.

Madison pulled himself off the ground. He stood and waited for the inevitable.

* * *

After a quick push, Williams slammed the van door. The van edged down the sloped road into the lake, which had flooded the road and bridge with spring runoff.

As the van sank deeper, the cold water seeped through the doors and touched Isabel's foot. She jerked and pulled away. She blinked her eyes, looked down at the water, and realized what was happening. A low gutteral moan started in her throat and erupted as a scream. She grabbed the key in the ignition and turned it. Nothing happened. The engine was submerged. She jerked off her seat belt, pulled on the door handle, and pushed and pounded on the door, but it would not budge. Water was up to the window now. When she pressed the button for the windows, nothing happened. The windows were electric and had no power.

Isabel turned to Jeagan and shook her. "Jeagan!" she screamed. "Please, Jeagan. You've got to help get us out of here." Jeagan slumped over in her seat. "Oh, my God!" Isabel prayed. "Please, God, no!"

* * *

The two patrol cars rounded the circular drive—tires spinning and gravel flying—and raced along the driveway and down the road behind the house.

Minutes later, a red Cadillac crested a hill and came toward them.

Roger squinted his eyes. "Who's that?"

"Could be her sister and that old black man could be the butler." Lieutenant Freshour jerked his steering wheel sideways in front of the Cadillac. Both men jumped out, followed by the deputy in the car behind them, and approached Agnes' car.

"Are you Agnes Harraway?" the deputy demanded.

Her voice calm, Agnes smiled at the men. "Why, yes. Can I help you?"

"Where is she?" Roger demanded.

"Do you mean my sister, Isabel?" Agnes said sweetly.

Roger grabbed the woman's jacket. "You know damn well who I mean. What have you done to Jeagan and your sister?"

Lieutenant Freshour pulled Roger's hand free from Agnes' jacket and jostled him away from the car. "I'll handle this." He placed his hands on the frame of the open window and leaned toward Agnes. "Make it easier on yourself, ma'am, and tell us where they are."

Wide-eyed, Agnes said, "Williams and I have been out looking for them. They left the house an hour ago and should have been back by now. My sister took Miss Christensen for a drive around the property."

"Don't give me that! What have you done with them?" Roger yelled.

* * *

Isabel continued to shake Jeagan. The van completely submerged and the water inside inched higher. She tried to open the door again, hoping she could somehow pull herself and Jeagan out of the van. The door still would not budge. As the cold, black water swirled around her waist, Isabel sobbed uncontrollably. She reached over to unfasten Jeagan's seat belt. After several attempts, she finally freed Jeagan. Isabel pulled on Jeagan's collar to keep her head above the rising water that was now at shoulder level. Isabel realized the water would soon be over their heads. "Please, God. Help us!" she screamed.

Roger scanned the area and spotted the lake at the far end of the road. He raced toward it. When he reached the water's edge, he pulled off his shoes and waded in until it was waist high. Then, he plunged in. He swam and groped his way through slimy weeds and floating debris. Nothing was visible in the murky water. When he could hold his breath no longer, he surfaced for a gulp of air and plunged in again. Moments later, as he forced himself deeper into the lake, his leg struck a large, solid object. He turned and felt for the object. It was the back of a van! He knew the women were inside. He swam to the driver's door and pulled on the handle. The door would not open. Inside he could hear someone thrashing wildly. He jerked on the door handle again and again. Finally, it opened. Although he desperately needed air himself, he grabbed the thrashing body, pulled the woman from the van, and pushed her toward the surface.

When he reached the surface, he realized the woman was Isabel. A deputy, who stood at the water's edge, dove in and swam toward Roger. He grabbed Isabel—weak and gasping and spitting up lake water—and pulled her back to shore.

"Jeagan!" Isabel cried between gasps for air.

Roger plunged in again. He swam back to the van and reached in the open door for Jeagan. He grabbed her arms and pulled her toward him, but her body would not move. Something held her back. Roger felt around and found that her skirt was caught. He jerked on the skirt and tore it free. Her body floated toward him. He pulled her from the van and pushed her toward the surface.

Lieutenant Freshour waded in and helped Roger pull Jeagan to shore, where Roger lifted her and carried her to a grassy area.

"She's not breathing," Roger said hoarsely as he carefully laid her on the ground. He pushed her hair away from her face as Lieutenant Freshour felt for a pulse. Panic rose from the pit of Roger's stomach when the lieutenant shook his head.

"I can't find a pulse," Lieutenant Freshour said.

Roger ignored the lieutenant and started CPR. "Come on, Jeagan," he said as he pumped her chest. "You can't die on me." Not this beautiful girl with the golden hair and heart to match. He had watched her commit a felony to try to help someone. She had to live.

Still coughing and shaking, Isabel watched—helpless. Tears slipped down her cheeks and mixed with the mud and sand smeared across her face and neck.

Chapter Twenty-Two

At four o'clock the next morning, Geoff Christensen hurried down the dimly lit hall of the intensive care unit of Oxford Community General Hospital. He had chartered a plane as soon as Roger had called the evening before. The sharp slap of Geoff's loafers echoed on the linoleum floor in the pre-dawn quietness. He stopped when he reached the bright white nurses station, but continued down the hall when he saw Roger in a waiting room at the end of the corridor. Geoff ignored the nurse who called after him and hurried on. As he neared the waiting area—with restful, pale blue vinyl walls and hung with pictures of pastoral lake scenes—he saw that Roger's hair was rumpled, he was unshaven, and he looked as if he had slept in his clothes. He sat slumped over with his elbows on his knees, a half-empty cup of coffee in his hands. He raised his head when Geoff entered the room.

Roger stood. "It's sure good to see you."

"How is she?" Geoff asked as he gripped Roger's hand and looked into his bloodshot eyes.

"She's still unconscious," Roger said as he ran his hand through his sandy-blond hair.

"Where's the doctor?" Geoff, his eyes red-rimmed and swollen, looked around for someone in charge.

"He was in a few minutes ago." Roger pointed in the direction of the glass doors that led to the Intensive Care Unit. "That's him in there. The guy with dark hair talking to the nurse." Roger walked toward the doors and opened them. He could see Jeagan through glass windows on the other side of the unit. Tubes ran in and out of her body.

"Dr. Hillman?" Roger said.

The doctor turned and acknowledged Roger.

"Jeagan's dad is here and would like to talk to you."

"I'll be right there." Dr. Scott Hillman signed the chart that the nurse held. He turned and strode toward the double doors.

"This is Jeagan's dad, Geoff Christensen," Roger said as the doctor approached the two men.

Geoff extended his hand to the doctor. "How's my daughter?"

"She received a hard blow to the back of her head and was under water for several minutes," Dr. Hillman said. "If it hadn't been for this man, we would've lost her. He kept working with her even after everyone else had given up."

"Can I see her?" Geoff said, his eyes pleading.

"She's still unconscious. Her breathing is labored, and we have her on oxygen. You can go in for a few minutes, but make it brief."

Dr. Hillman led Geoff to his only child's room. His eyes filled with tears the minute he saw Jeagan's slender frame under the thin, white blanket. Wires and tubes seemed to protrude from all parts of her body. He pulled a chair to the side of her bed, sat down, and took Jeagan's hand in both of his. He bent his head and touched his lips to her cool, white hand.

"I'm so sorry," he whispered. "If only I'd listened to you. If your mother were still alive, she would've helped you. She was never too busy for you—like I've been for most of your life." Tears rolled down his face and fell onto Jeagan's hand. Geoff touched her pale face and noticed the raspy sounds coming from her lungs.

After several minutes, Dr. Hillman re-entered the room and touched Geoff on the shoulder. "You'd better go now. We'll let you know if there's a change."

Geoff wearily pulled himself from the chair. After he wiped his eyes with a handkerchief, he went back to the waiting room. Roger and the doctor followed him. Geoff dropped into a plaid armchair. "What can I do?"

"There's nothing you can do now except hope and pray that she is strong enough to come around," Dr. Hillman said. "We're helping her body as much as we can but the rest is up to her."

After the doctor left the room, Roger said, "I'm really sorry, Geoff. If I'd only kept a low profile and not gotten caught by the house detective…"

Geoff shook his head. "I don't blame you. I blame myself. If I'd been there for her when she tried to get through to me, none of this would have happened."

"Well, we can't do anything now but wait. That's the worst part." Roger glanced at his watch. "Have you eaten lately?"

Geoff sighed. "No. Just coffee. I haven't even thought about food since you called last night."

"Why don't we go down to the cafeteria and have some breakfast?" Roger said. "I hear the food's decent."

Geoff rose from the chair. "I guess it beats sitting here helpless." He followed Roger out of the room and along the hall to the nurses' station.

A fresh-faced, young nurse stopped writing in the chart she held and looked up from the white formica counter as the men approached. "May I help you?"

"This is Jeagan Christensen's dad, Geoff."

The nurse nodded and smiled.

"We're going to the cafeteria for some breakfast," Roger said. "Will you call us if there is any change in Jeagan?"

"I certainly will, Mr. Sanderlin," the nurse said. "When you return to the floor, be sure to check in with us so we'll know where to find you."

"Thank you. We'll do that." Roger walked with Geoff to the elevator. They rode to the first floor in silence. "I believe the cafeteria is this way," Roger said. He indicated the corridor to their right as they stepped off the elevator and walked noiselessly down the carpeted hall.

* * *

Jeagan stirred and moaned. Movement caused spikes of shooting pain through her head. She touched it, expecting it to be twice its normal size. It was normal except for a hard lump on the back, which was bandaged. When she opened her eyes, she looked around and noticed that she wore a blue hospital gown, had all kinds of instruments attached to her, and was in a hospital room. Where was she and how had she gotten here?

Slowly, the door to her room opened. She heard a thump against the doorframe. New pain shot through her head as she turned toward the door. She moaned again, closed her eyes, and then brought her hand to her head.

"You're awake," someone whispered.

Jeagan opened her eyes again and watched as Isabel, in a blue hospital gown and robe, steered her wheelchair into the room.

Jeagan forced a half smile. Isabel's short, gray hair stood out at odd angles. "Hello, Isabel. What happened?" Jeagan heard a quiet drone as Isabel's electric wheelchair moved toward the bed.

The door opened again. "You're awake," a young nurse with maple-colored hair said as she entered the room.

Holding her head, Jeagan said, "Is that all anybody can say to me?"

The nurse moved to the bed and reached for Jeagan's wrist to take her pulse. "How are you feeling?"

"Death warmed over doesn't even come close," Jeagan mumbled.

After she looked into Jeagan's eyes and took her blood pressure, the nurse said, "Let me get you something for that pain." She patted Jeagan's arm. "I'll be right back, honey."

Isabel wheeled herself close to the bed, reached over, and touched Jeagan's hand. "I'm so sorry to have gotten you involved in all this...this terrible mess."

"What happened to me? The last thing I remember is leaving the Peabody with Madison." Anxious, Jeagan tried to sit up but the pain brought tears to her eyes. "Is Madison all right?"

"You really don't remember, do you?" Isabel said.

Jeagan tried to lift her head again, but the pain was too intense. She sank back on the pillow, her pale face framed by her straggly, golden-brown hair. "Tell me, Isabel. Is he all right?"

"I hate to have to tell you this, but my sister and Williams tried to kill us."

Jeagan's eyes flew open. "Oh, my God!" She looked down at Isabel and grabbed her hand. "Oh, Isabel. Now I remember. I called out to Madison to help us, but he wouldn't." Slowly events reconstructed themselves in her mind as a fit of coughing seized her.

"Just relax." Isabel reached for a pitcher of water and poured some into a glass. She placed a straw in the glass and put it up to Jeagan's mouth. "Here. Drink some water."

Jeagan sipped through the straw. "Thanks," she said when she drank all she could. "Thomas and Agnes made us get in the van and drove us to a lake, didn't they?"

Isabel nodded. "Yes. Then Agnes hit you with a gun. You were unconscious when they pushed the van down the road into the water."

"Into the lake?" Jeagan asked.

"Yes. I tried and tried to wake you, but not even the cold water and shaking you helped. I thought we were dead when the water reached the roof of the van. It was horrible." Tears formed in Isabel's eyes. I tried to stay calm, but when the water covered my head…"

"Good God!" Jeagan tried to raise herself again, but lay back on the pillow and covered her eyes with her arm. "My head is killing me," she moaned. After a moment, she said, "How did we get out? You couldn't have gotten us out of that van."

Isabel pulled a tissue from the box on the nightstand and dabbed at her eyes. "Roger pulled us out. He got me out before I passed out. It's a wonder I didn't drown both of us the way I fought to get to the surface after he managed to get the door open. He grabbed my hands, pulled me out, and then pushed me up. A policeman was there when I got to the surface. He held me while I coughed up the lake and got my breath. Then, he helped me to the bank while Roger went back in after you."

"Who's Roger?" Jeagan asked.

The door to the room opened. Isabel turned to see who had entered. She smiled. "That's Roger."

"The guy who was stalking me!" Jeagan said. She stared at the sandy-haired man while she held her throbbing head.

Roger grinned. "Not stalking–baby-sitting."

Indignant, Jeagan said, "Excuse me?"

Roger laughed. "It's good to see you're awake and sassy. That's a good sign."

"Who are you and why were you following me?" Jeagan demanded.

Roger held the door open and looked down the hall. Geoff had stopped at the nurses station. Roger motioned to him.

Geoff ran toward Jeagan's room. "This is the reason I followed you." Roger held the door open wider as Geoff Christensen stepped inside the room.

"Dad!"

"Oh, Jeagan," Geoff strode across the room. He took his daughter's hand, "I was so scared…How do you feel?" He gently pushed her hair away from her face and kissed her cheek.

Jeagan squeezed her dad's hand. Her eyes overflowed. "A lot better now that you're here."

"Roger called me after the accident. I chartered the fastest plane I could find."

"Roger called you?" Jeagan turned her head, with a groan, toward Roger, who leaned against the wall with his hands stuffed in his pockets.

"I sent Roger here to keep you out of trouble," Geoff said.

Roger shook his head. "Guess I didn't do a very good job of that."

Isabel turned toward Roger. "You saved her life. That should count for something."

"I'm not thinking very clearly," Jeagan said and looked at Roger, "but I guess I owe you an apology…and a thank you."

161

Roger grinned. "My pleasure."

Jeagan held her head and remembered. She looked down at Isabel. "The baby…Alan. Isabel, what about Alan?"

Isabel's face brightened. "I contacted my attorney this morning. He said he will use every means possible to find Alan." Her eyes glistened with tears. "Thank you so much for all you went through for me and…for telling me about Alan. I still don't understand how you knew…"

Jeagan squeezed Isabel's hand tighter. "I don't understand it either. Maybe Alan's spirit used me to reach you and tell you what really happened to him, or maybe I did a little time traveling back to 1944."

A wistful smile crossed Isabel's face. "I wish I could travel back to 1944 and change things."

"I wish you could too," Jeagan said.

Chapter Twenty-Three

A week later, Jeagan unlocked the door to her condominium, passed through the kitchen where she dropped her keys on the green granite bar, and entered the family room. She walked over to two-story windows that faced the Rockies and drew the cream-colored drapes, edged in green and peach, to let in the brilliant Colorado sunshine. She looked around at her comfortable green, peach, and cream sofas and antique tables. Home never looked so good.

She continued down the carpeted hallway past the guest room to her bedroom. She set her handbag on her desk when she reached the bedroom, but jerked it away again, out of habit, and placed it on the vanity in the bathroom. When she opened her handbag, she pulled out her airline ticket and started to throw it away when something fell out of it. She reached down and retrieved a card. It was the business card of the woman she had met on the plane, Candice Franklin. Jeagan smiled at the thought of the kind, attractive woman who had listened so willingly to her problems with her dad and Brandon. That was all behind her now, Jeagan thought. She dropped the card, along with her airline ticket, into the waste can. Then, she looked at herself in the vanity mirror.

"I wonder if...?" She grinned at herself in the mirror and then bent to retrieve Candice's business card from the waste can. Maybe she would give Candice a call when she returned to Denver and arrange to have lunch, and maybe she would arrange for her dad to join them. An attractive, friendly widow might be just the thing for him.

This decided, Jeagan walked over to her desk. "You sure put me through a lot of heartache and pain," she said, as she pulled out the chair and tentatively sat down. "Now, give me back my life." She tensed, squeezed her eyes shut, and waited for a wave of dizziness to overtake her.

After several long minutes, nothing happened. She experienced no dizziness, she heard no sounds, and best of all, she saw nothing. Jeagan relaxed. Life was back to normal. "Thank you, Lord," she whispered as she looked out the window at the clear, paint-box blue Colorado sky. "I have my life back, I have my dad back, I have a new friend in Memphis…"

The loud jangling of the telephone in the quiet condo startled Jeagan. She walked over to her nightstand to answer it. "Hello?"

"So, you're home?"

A slow grin spread across Jeagan's face. "You're the private investigator, you should know."

"Oh, I see we're still sassy," Roger said.

"Always."

"Hmm. I see. So, that's how it's going to be?"

Jeagan laughed. "Good to hear your voice."

"Good to hear yours too. Sorry I had to leave you guys in Memphis, but I had to get back to testify in court for…for one of the big telecom companies here."

"Oh, can't tell me the name of your client," Jeagan teased. "Hush, hush stuff?"

"Well…not exactly," Roger said. "It's just that I don't make a habit of discussing my cases. Uh, how's the head?"

"Much better. Dr. Hillman tried to keep me a couple more days, but I'd had enough of being away from Denver. I missed the mountains and then there's my job. I need to get back to work."

"Speaking of work, how would you like to help me out with a job I just got this morning? It might require some travel to Seattle or Vancouver…"

"Seattle! I love Seattle," Jeagan said. She sat on her bed. "Tell me more."

"Well, I don't want to take you away from your job at Caldwell & Ottonello, but this assignment could use a woman's touch, especially a woman who is as tenacious as you."

"That's the nicest thing you've ever said to me, Mr. P.I."

"I could say a lot nicer things, but I probably won't...for now. Anyway, I've been given a large expense account for this job and...well, I'd like your help if you can take some time away from your job."

"You're serious, aren't you?" Jeagan said.

"Dead serious."

"What kind of work are you talking about?"

"Looking for a missing child."

"Oh," Jeagan said. She grabbed her stomach feeling as if a cold, lead weight had just hit the bottom of it.

"Are you up for it?" Roger asked.

"I'd like to think about it before I commit one way or..."

"Have dinner with me tonight and we can discuss it. Okay?"

Jeagan said nothing for a moment. "How old is the child?"

"About fifty," Roger said. Jeagan could hear the smile in his voice.

Jeagan's breath caught in her throat. "You don't mean...?"

"I do mean. Isabel has hired me to find Alan."

"But, I thought her attorney was handling the case."

"He is but apparently all the records of the adoption were lost during a flood in Dovington ten years ago."

"Then why did you tell me that I might have to travel to Seattle or Vancouver? How would you know to start looking there?

"Isabel went through a box of her father's personal papers after he died. At the time, nothing in the box appeared important, but she never got around to throwing them out. Anyway, she looked through the papers again yesterday and found a letter from an attorney in Seattle dated April of 1945."

"What did the letter say?"

"The letter said that a check for ten thousand dollars was enclosed."

"Do you think that Isabel's father sold Alan to a couple in Seattle?"

"That's exactly what I think. I've checked in Seattle and the attorney is deceased, but I believe that with a little digging..."

"...that we can find the connection to Alan," Jeagan said, completing Roger's thought.

"That's what I'm thinking. Are you in?"

Jeagan smiled to herself. "Nothing would give me greater pleasure." She looked at her watch. "What time should I be ready?"

"I knew I could count on you. I'll see you at seven."

Jeagan hung up the phone and fell back on the bed. Her mind started to buzz with things she needed to do. She had planned to start back to work tomorrow, but now—this was much more important than writing proposals. If she and Roger could find Alan for Isabel...She jumped up from her bed. She would have to call Lorin and tell him that she would not be back to work for a while. Hopefully, things were slow enough that he could do without her for a while longer. Then, she looked at Candice's business card. She slipped the edge of it under her nightstand lamp. When she got back in town, she would give Candice a call and set up a meeting with her dad.

She got up from the bed and walked into the bathroom. She looked at herself in the vanity mirror and grinned. "And you thought things were getting back to normal..."

About the Author

Jonna Turner—a former Memphian—lives in Denver, Colorado with her husband, Bill—a FedEx pilot—and their golden retrievers, Savannah and Shiloh.

Jonna's background includes radio scripts for Art Linkletter's *The ART of Positive Thinking*, national and local fiction awards, and feature articles for a newspaper. In addition to *The Desk*, Jonna has written a book of short stories entitled *Stories from the Heart*, and a mystery/time travel novel, *The Other Side of Time*. She is currently at work on her next mystery novel, *New Pictures of an Old Murder*.

Printed in the United States
943500001B